"You do understand that you came driving into my family room, right?"

Being this close to her, he noticed the cuts on her face and smudge of mud on her cheek. Under all that dirt lurked a stunning woman. Big eyes and a sassy mouth. It was a killer combination that kicked his lust into high gear.

"I'm sorry about that." She had the decency to wince.

"You're sorry?"

"I can barely stand, my skull feels like it's about to break open and I'm pretty sure I have someone else's blood in my hair."

"And?"

"Then there's the part where someone is trying to kill me and I have no idea why. So I'm sorry if you find me unpleasant or ungrateful, but I just don't have it in me at the moment to care."

Spunk. He didn't want to, but he liked it. "Fair enough."

HELENKAY DIMON

GUNS AND THE GIRL NEXT DOOR

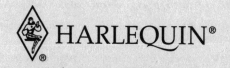

HARLEQUIN®

TORONTO • NEW YORK • LONDON
AMSTERDAM • PARIS • SYDNEY • HAMBURG
STOCKHOLM • ATHENS • TOKYO • MILAN • MADRID
PRAGUE • WARSAW • BUDAPEST • AUCKLAND

Thank you to Denise Zaza for suggesting I try a miniseries. That led to the Recovery Project and five of my all-time favorite heroes.

Recycling programs
for this product may
not exist in your area.

ISBN-13: 978-0-373-74575-3

GUNS AND THE GIRL NEXT DOOR

Copyright © 2011 by HelenKay Dimon

ABOUT THE AUTHOR

Award-winning author HelenKay Dimon spent twelve years in the most unromantic career ever—divorce lawyer. After dedicating all that effort to helping people terminate relationships, she is thrilled to deal in happy endings and write romance novels for a living. Now her days are filled with gardening, writing, reading and spending time with her family in and around San Diego. HelenKay loves hearing from readers, so stop by her website at www.helenkaydimon.com and say hello.

Books by HelenKay Dimon

HARLEQUIN INTRIGUE
1196—UNDER THE GUN*
1214—NIGHT MOVES
1254—GUNS AND THE GIRL NEXT DOOR*

*Mystery Men

CAST OF CHARACTERS

Holden Price—Undercover Recovery Project agent Holden doesn't know what to think when a mystery woman drives her car right through his front door. But when gunmen come hunting, Holden sure knows what to do—protect her.

Mia Landers—She changed her job and her life and now someone wants Mia dead. Running for her life, she crashes into Holden. He's solid and strong and could be the very reason everyone suddenly wants her dead.

Bram Walters—A wealthy and powerful congressman. He's Mia's boss...is he also behind a web of corruption that's left several women dead?

Trevor Walters—Bram's brother and a highly regarded businessman. On the surface he's legitimate, but things aren't always what they seem.

Rod Lehman—Holden's missing boss. Rod took an off-the-books job looking into irregularities in the Witness Security Program and now he's gone. Holden wants to believe Rod's alive, but the evidence is pointing in another direction.

Ned Zimmer—Mia's ex keeps showing up exactly where he shouldn't be. Mia changed her life to get away from Ned, but he's found her again and isn't leaving.

Luke Hathaway—The interim head of the Recovery Project and Holden's friend, Luke has vowed to keep his agents safe, even if that means protecting Luke from Mia.

Chapter One

Ignoring the burning in her thighs and tears stinging her eyes, Mia Landers ran. Her arms pumped up and down, propelling her through the thick woods. She had to reach her car before he caught her.

Dead leaves crunched under her feet, drowning out the pounding heartbeat in her ears. When stray branches scratched against her face, she pushed them out of the way and concentrated on staying steady on the patches of dirt beneath her.

The path had been lost to time and the night was pure black, but she refused to give up. Not when she could hear him screaming her name in a crazed frenzy behind her.

She blocked that out. Slam the door, shove the key in and drive away as fast as possible. That was the plan. She just had to make it to the car alive first.

"Mia!"

His angry voice boomed around her, bouncing through the trees in this open area of Virginia…. Were they even in Virginia anymore? She had no idea.

The past hour played in her mind like a movie gone wrong. Her boss had said to drive and she did. Lost in spitting anger, he had rapid-fired commands at her and she followed them. They left the safety of her car, got out and walked.

Then he lost his mind.

Everything that came after moved in a blur. He had lunged, his face twisted and red with fury. She kicked and punched. The second he fell to his knees she took off. Problem was hitting him in the side of the head with her purse had only slowed him down.

Even now thudding steps rang out behind her, gaining and threatening, as his heavy breathing drew closer. She tried to pick up speed but the heels of her sensible pumps slid, throwing her off balance every time her foot struck the muddy ground. The only good news was that she wore a pantsuit that day. If she had picked out her usual pencil skirt that morning, she'd be dead.

The cold air burned as she forced it down her rough throat. Not that she could feel the chill on her skin. It didn't matter that she'd taken off her blazer. Her body had gone numb. But she could see the car. It sat about a hundred feet away.

The death grip on her keys pressed indentations into her palms, but she refused to let go. She'd already lost her cell phone when she dropped her purse. Scrambling around in the dark for the keys was not an option.

Just when she thought she'd never be free of the claustrophobic woods, she broke into the clearing and sprinted across the grass to the parked car. Unable to stop her momentum, her midsection slammed into the side of the sedan with a loud thump. The air rushed out of her lungs on impact. She doubled over, gasping as she struggled for breath.

Then she saw him standing there. Staring. Blood clumped on the side of his head and eyes wild with rage. The rip in the shoulder of his black suit jacket and scratches on his cheek gave testimony to the battle she'd fought before struggling out of his grasp.

Her key chain jangled in her hand, breaking through her stupor. She fumbled as her heart galloped, glancing away from him only long enough to hit the button for the automatic locks to throw the door open.

Her whole body trembled as she fell into the seat and locked her body in. Blood raced through her veins as the sound of her heavy breathing filled the car.

Like a vicious demon, dark and evil, he descended on her, roaring as he came. The heels of his hands slammed against her window. "Get out!"

She flinched at the mix of pounding and yelling, fearing every minute that he would break through the glass and grab her.

"Mia!"

She didn't wait. The key turned just as he struck his fists against the hood of the car. Banging crashed in around her. Ducking, she waited for the metal to cave in. When it held, she swallowed back the panic building in her throat.

Fingers wrapped around the steering wheel, back hunched over, she hit the gas. The engine revved and tires spun.

Still he wouldn't let up. He beat his fists against the car. With the pedal pressed hard into the floor, the back end finally swung around and knocked right into him. His eyes grew huge just before he yelped. His fingernails screeched against her window as he went down.

She didn't check to see if he got up again.

To gain traction she lifted her foot off the gas and forced her thigh to ease back down again. With control restored, she took a quick look around for the nearest exit through the trees. Her memory jumbled. She saw only a dirt area and surrounding woods.

Blinking, she tried to remember how she got in there. When she focused again, he stood right in front of her car.

Warped anger rolled off of him in waves. An arm hung loose at his side. His face screwed up in a mask of insane fury.

She ran the car right into him. Aimed for his stomach and gunned it.

His body disappeared under the front of her car. To avoid rolling over him, she backed up and then maneuvered the vehicle around in a circle. Dust kicked up around the shaking metal as her tires squealed. With a quick glance in her rearview window at his crumpled and unmoving form, she took off, refusing to feel a second's guilt.

She drove without a destination, fueled by adrenaline and terror and little else. Blackness enveloped her from all sides. The area lacked street signs and lights. Nothing marked the way or pointed toward civilization.

Why did he bring her out here? She turned

the question over in her mind. The possibilities raced by her.

To keep from crashing, she forced her brain back to the task at hand. She needed to concentrate on the escape and the Y in the dirt road in front of her. Nothing felt familiar. Anxiety bubbled up in her stomach. Biting her lower lip, she closed her eyes and chose the right branch at random.

About a half mile in, her car rattled and dipped as she drove over rocks and through divots. She didn't remember the road being this rough. She didn't remember anything except her heart pulsing hard enough to set off a knocking in her head.

The steering wheel shifted from side to side and she clenched her fists tighter in a futile attempt to keep control. On the verge of giving up hope, she made out the shadow of a building in the distance. Lights. If it was a hallucination, it was a welcome one.

Holding on tighter, she aimed for a driveway, anything to indicate life, a phone and the police—any order would do so long as she got help and found safety. Her shoulders relaxed and her breaths came more easily.

The clunk took her by surprise. The back end of her car went one way and the front another. The bleak night hid the pattern of the road. She didn't know what she ran over, but it was something. Something big that had her back tires bouncing against the ground and the steering wheel slipping further out of her sure grasp.

The structure, a small house, came up fast. One minute it loomed in the distance. The next she was on top of it. Before she could hit the brakes she smashed through a wooden fence. And kept right on going.

She pumped the brakes. The car slowed but refused to stop. She hit the pedal and slid her fingers over the console in search of the emergency brake. But it was too late. She glanced up in time to see the cabin's front door crash right into the hood.

Chapter Two

Holden Price leaned his head back against his couch and threw his baseball in the air for what felt like the hundredth time. Much more of this and his catching hand would go numb.

Being on paid leave was not his idea of a good time. More like torture.

Up until two months ago he'd worked undercover with the Recovery Project, an off-the-books government agency fronting as an antiques salvage operation. He found missing people for a living, those on the run who didn't want to be found and those who were desperate for rescue.

One case gone wrong and pencil-pushing higher-ups disbanded the Project and subpoenaed his boss, Rod Lehman, to Capitol Hill for top-secret congressional subcommittee hearings. It all sounded like a load of bureaucratic crap to Holden.

He'd spent his twenties in the army and the first four years of his thirties at the Project. Without the routine of work the past few weeks dragged. He couldn't remember ever being this bored.

The ball thumped against his palm before he whipped it into the air again. The seam turned end over end as it traveled halfway to his family-room ceiling. It ran out of oomph and began falling back down just as the lights on his outside alarm system flickered to life on the panel next to the door.

Shrill beeps filled the room and kept right on cycling. When tires squealed outside the large double window across from him, Holden lifted his head and saw the blinding headlights weaving and shifting straight up his lawn.

The sights and sounds refused to register in his brain. By design, his cabin sat in the middle of nowhere. He dealt with dangerous people and life-threatening situations. The unsettling mix had convinced him long ago to set up a sanctuary, a place of peace known only to a few friends who also happened to be gun-carrying colleagues.

And now someone was violating the safety zone he'd created, using more than three thousand pounds of automobile as a weapon to do it.

He scrambled off the cushion and grabbed for the gun in his side table. He hit the floor on his right shoulder just as the sedan smacked through his front door. The crashing boom rattled the cabin's foundation.

The wood creaked and splintered. Studs crumbled. The lights dimmed as the exposed wires fell from the smashed ceiling panels and pushed the electricity nearly to the breaking point.

With dust flying and pieces of furniture scattered everywhere, Holden sat still, his back to what was left of the couch and his gun aimed at the bowed head in the front seat of the car. Long blond hair mixed with the broken windshield glass even as the white-knuckled grip continued its hold on the steering wheel.

His attacker was a she.

And possibly dead.

She also didn't have an air bag, which he found odd. Not that any part of the past two minutes had been normal.

Slow and as quiet as a man of his size could manage, he jumped to his feet. The muzzle didn't waver. Neither did his stare. If she moved, he'd be ready to shoot.

Glass crunched under his feet as he approached the front of the car. The house alarm blared, but Holden tuned it out. His focus centered on her. Whoever "her" was.

"Lift your head." He issued the order in his best *you're a dead woman* tone.

Nothing.

To keep from going deaf, he headed for the alarm. Shifting around the side of the car and keeping his body square with the mystery driver, he reached out to disarm the thing. He lifted his hand and felt nothing but the cool March night air.

Snow hadn't fallen in Northern Virginia this week, but the crisp smell signaled what could be a final winter blast. Now that he lacked a front wall, that was going to be a problem.

Glancing down, he traced his foot through the debris littering what was once a shiny hardwood floor. No sign of the panel, but he did spy his keys. As he leaned down to grab the chain, the driver's head popped up.

She screamed loud enough to make his ears shrivel.

The shriek echoed inside his brain, drowning out the annoying sound of the alarm. In two seconds, he hit the code on his key chain to stop the electronic screeching. At the same time, he leveled the gun at the woman's forehead in an attempt to quiet her.

"Stop," he ordered.

"Wh-what…?"

"Do not move." When she tried to open her door, he lifted his foot and kicked it shut on her again.

"Hey!"

"You're not listening. Stay right there."

Her hand shook as she pressed it to her forehead. "What are you doing?"

"Setting the ground rules."

The skin at corners of her eyes wrinkled. "What?"

"This is my house."

She shook her head and then grabbed it. "I don't understand," she said in a voice rough with what sounded like pain.

He didn't know what to believe. Hard to trust a woman who used his family room as a parking lot.

"Yeah, we'll see about that," he mumbled.

Her gaze shot to the gun and then back at his face. "Who are you?"

The look of wild-eyed panic had him thinking she might actually not know, but he wasn't taking the chance. "We're going to focus on my questions first. What are you doing here?"

"I…" Turning her head with a careful slowness that suggested an injury, she looked around the inside of the car. She glanced up and over the wheel as if noticing for the first time the damage around her. "Did I crash?"

The stuttering tone and dropped jaw were nice touches. Added to the sham.

Holden didn't buy any of it. "Uh, yeah. That's one way of putting it."

"Where am I?"

"In the middle of my family room. Now, tell me your name."

"Mia Landers." She shifted her upper body and winced.

His elbows locked. "Stay right there."

"I need to get up."

"Are you hurt, Mia?"

She bit her lower lip. "I don't know."

Not exactly the answer he expected. "It's a simple question. Yes or no?"

"Not really."

He gave her two options and she picked a third. Interesting. "What does that mean?"

"I'm kind of numb."

Shock. Assassin or bad driver, he still wasn't

sure but he did know she probably needed medical attention. "Open the door nice and slow."

She stared down at her lap. "I can't…"

From the glassy stare it looked as if his unwanted guest was losing it and fast. He stepped closer and followed her gaze to her legs. Minimal blood and room to move around under the dash, as far as he could tell. Just in case the stunned unblinking stare was a ruse, he didn't let up.

"Let's get out now." He slipped his hand under the handle and opened the door for her. When she tried to get out without taking off her seat belt, he reached in and did the deed for her. "Here you go."

Hands shaking, hair hanging in front of her eyes, she turned to the side and got one foot out of the car. On her first attempt to get up her knees buckled and her butt hit the leather seat hard.

Taking a long look, visually searching every part of her he could see for weapons, Holden gave in and tucked his gun in the small of his back. As gently as possible, he slid one arm between her back and the seat and tugged her out of the car, doing a subtle pat down in the process. A person couldn't be too safe in a situation like this.

Her legs wobbled and every inch of her trembled, but she managed to stumble to her feet with him for support. "Oh, man."

"You okay?" he asked when he had her on her feet, standing near what once was his front door.

"I think so. My head hurts but not too bad." She wiped an unsteady hand through her hair. Her fingers snagged on leaves and a few pieces of cubed glass. "How did I get here?"

"I was wondering that same thing." He guided her to his couch that was just about the only piece of nearby furniture to survive the crash, and only half of that was usable.

He also took a second to size up his opponent. Late twenties, five-seven or so, slim with an innocent round face that easily could be telling a lie or two.

She probably needed a glass of water and an ambulance, but he wasn't ready to offer either yet. No one wandered around these dense woods at night. Beautiful blondes with bright green eyes rarely came out this way unless he invited them, and that didn't happen all that frequently either. He used hotels in

D.C. for that sort of thing, preferring to keep his private life at home very private.

"Tell me why you were out here," he said.

"Where?"

"On my property." Except for a historic estate about ten miles away, he was the only one out there.

Two miles of wooded land separated him from the main road. He used to think that was enough space. Now he wasn't so sure.

"I was..." Her eyes grew huge as her mouth fell flat. "Oh, my God."

"What?"

"I have to—"

She tried to stand up, but he anchored her next to him on the cushions. "Whoa."

"You don't understand." Her gaze darted around the room. Her hands were in constant motion as if the energy inside her had sparked to life and wanted to get moving.

He soothed a hand over her shoulder. "Explain it to me."

"I have to call the police."

"Why?"

"The accident."

The last thing he wanted was a squad of police cars swarming all over his property. If he had to, then yes, but he wanted to put it off until he understood exactly who Mia was and why she was in his house.

"Did you fall asleep at the wheel?"

"No."

She sounded as if she had her full memory back now. "Was anyone in the car with you?"

She patted the pockets of her ripped and smudged pants. "It's here somewhere."

Watching her move, he still couldn't tell what was happening. "What are you looking for?"

"My cell. I have to call the police and my office."

"Mia, listen to me—"

"Now I remember. I dropped it."

He put one of his hands over hers. "Doesn't matter."

She stopped shifting and babbling and stared up at him. "Wait, what did you say?"

He could barely follow her zigzagging conversation. "Tell me what happened out there."

She swallowed hard enough for him to see her throat move. "I hit someone."

That's what he feared. He had not one but two victims running around his property. "So, there was a car accident?"

She toed the pile of what used to be his coffee table and now barely qualified as kindling. "Look around you."

"I meant before you came sailing through the window."

"Not exactly."

"But you're saying there's a person out there who needs help." He had some training, the usual military survival stuff but not much more. If the injuries were serious, he'd need help.

"No." Her voice sounded far away, almost dreamy.

"Mia?"

"He's dead." Her eyes focused, looking clear for the first time. "I killed him."

Holden had no idea who the "he" was or what was happening, but the lady seemed to need soothing and no one else was there to do it, so he tried. "I'm sure that's not true."

She stared him down. "I hope it is."

Chapter Three

Mia sat there, looking into a pair of ice-blue eyes and wondering why the guy just happened to be holding a gun when she drove through his wall.

"You're not making sense," the mystery man said.

That probably had something to do with being terrified. If her body shook any harder, her brain might start rattling. It was bad enough her back teeth kept knocking together. She also had to deal with the pain above her eyes and bones that had turned to jelly.

First, she got attacked by her usually boring boss. That one still didn't make sense. Now a guy with a scowl harsh enough to make her swallow her tongue in panic sat just inches away. With his coal-black hair and broad shoulders, he reminded her of some of the secret-service teams that walked through the

Rayburn House Office Building where she worked.

This guy had an air of danger to him. The muscles straining under the sleeves of his black T-shirt should have scared her, but he didn't give off that serial-killer vibe. Not that she knew how killers acted in these situations.

Right now, the only confirmed killer in the room was her. "He attacked me. Wouldn't stop."

"Who?"

The scene ran through her mind. Crazed eyes. Mumbled accusations. "He wanted me dead."

"Let me try this again—who?" The mystery man moved his hand to her arm.

She stared down at his long fingers and tried not to flinch. If he was dangerous, she didn't want to tick him off. She'd had enough of that for one evening. "What's your name?"

This time he didn't answer a question with one of his own. "Holden Price."

Nothing about that name gave her insight into who he was or how much he might want to hurt her. A solid name. Of course, so was Ted Bundy.

She needed a phone and reinforcements, preferably the type that wore badges and carried bigger guns than Holden. Knowing she was finally safe also would be a relief.

"Now," he said. "Let's skip to the part where you tell me about this other person."

She was more concerned with knowing everything about the potential threat in front of her. "You live here?"

Holden exhaled with just enough exasperation to let her know his patience was wearing thin. "I did until your recent redecorating, but I'm not the issue here. You are."

"I need to call the police."

Holden didn't move. "Tell me who you think you killed. Give me his name."

No harm in sharing that information. Everyone would know soon anyway. You couldn't kill someone of her boss's stature without making the news.

"Bram Walters," she said.

Holden's face fell. He actually went from looking frustrated to looking confused. "As in Congressman Bram Walters?"

"Same one."

Holden's gaze roamed over her face. "I don't recognize you."

Maybe the headache was the cause, but that was a comment that didn't fit. "Why would you?"

"I know Walters."

Not possible. She'd remember Holden. A guy who looked like him didn't walk into the congressional office without every single girl fluffing her hair and practicing her smile. Put a suit on this man and he'd still have the Tall, Dark and Devastating thing down.

"I'm one of Congressman Walters's legislative assistants," she said.

"In the D.C. office?"

She didn't understand Holden's obsession with her employment. His questions swam around in her head until she thought her skull would explode. "I've been there about two months."

"And now you think you killed the man you work for." Holden said the words nice and slow, hovering over each one.

"I ran him over."

"With your car." That comment took even longer for Holden to get out.

"Well, yeah."

"You're saying Walters was at my house."

She pressed a hand against her head to keep it from falling forward into her lap. "In the area."

Holden blew out a long breath. "Interesting."

"If I didn't kill him it wasn't for a lack of trying."

This time the corner of Holden's mouth kicked up in a smile. "I'd recommend you phrase that differently when you talk with the police."

Police. Trials. The press. This was all bad. The head spinning picked up speed. "I can't believe this."

"Me either."

It wasn't all that difficult to pick up on the shock in Holden's voice. Crossing him off the serial-killer list had proved a bit easier in the past few minutes. If he wanted to hurt her, he would have done it by now. Maybe he was the reclusive type, but he didn't strike her as a threat.

That realization slowed the runaway drumming of her heart. Well, it did until he got up and she got a close-up view of the gun balanced in the waistband of his pants.

"Where are you going?" she asked.

He shot her an expression that suggested she wasn't too bright. "To look for Walters."

"Why?"

Holden's eyes widened at that. "In case he's still alive and needs help."

"You can't." She jumped up and grabbed

Holden's arm, ignoring the tossing and turning in her stomach.

"Why is that?"

"My boss is dangerous." And the last thing she needed was a second round with him.

Guilt washed over her every time the image of the Congressman falling under her car replayed in her mind. Not that she'd had a choice. In a contest between them over who would live, she'd rather think of her boss as dead.

"Walters wears a suit and sits behind a desk all day making decisions without regard to the facts." Holden removed her fingers. "Trust me, I'm not afraid of him."

She focused in on Holden's comment. Blocked out everything else. "That's a pretty specific impression."

"I know politicians."

She didn't buy that explanation. Headache or not, this was something else. Something deeper and more personal. "I'm getting the sense you know this congressman."

"If you're right about killing him, we should be using the past tense."

She felt the need to defend her actions. "He went insane out there."

"Which brings me to my biggest question."

Holden slipped the gun out of his pants and held it at his side. "Why were you on my property with Walters?"

Seeing the weapon brought the panic rushing back and the searing headache right behind. It screamed along her senses, paralyzing her. "I don't know."

"Try again."

"I don't."

Holden shifted the gun behind him and leaned down until they were eye to eye. "Mia, I'm not playing around here. I want the truth."

Law enforcement. She'd bet her life on it. She knew the beast. The way he repeated her name. The steady tone to his voice. She'd dated a cop for two years. Holden had the same calm assurance. He oozed control and confidence.

And he handled that gun like a pro.

"The Congressman drove me out here, kept asking me who I was working for—"

Holden held up his free hand. "I thought you worked for him."

"I do…did. I actually don't know what happens now that he's dead."

"We'll go with the assumption he's very

much alive. If so, I don't get the comment about you working for someone else."

"Neither did I. The Congressman wanted to know what I was looking for in the system." The man had screamed it at her. That memory hadn't faded one bit. "I have no idea what he was talking about."

"System?"

"His personal computer. He keeps a laptop in the office. The only thing I can think of is he thought I broke into it for some reason."

A strange look flashed on Holden's face. Before she could decipher it, the expression disappeared. He morphed back into big-man-blank-look mode.

"Did you?" he asked.

"Why would I?"

"Why would you drive through my house?" He gestured around the room. "See? There are many questions that need answering here."

"If you say so."

"I do, but right now we're going outside."

"No." Smart women did not go running around in the dark with strange men. They also didn't race back into trouble once they'd escaped it. "Definitely not."

From the frown it was clear Holden didn't care for her refusal one bit. "Excuse me?"

"The police."

"You can keep saying that but it's not going to happen. Not until I know what we're dealing with here."

She glanced around for a phone, careful not to move her head too fast. The thing must be under her car because she didn't see it. "A dead member of the House of Representatives. That's kind of a big deal, don't you think?"

"I'm not the one who killed him."

She stopped. "You're not funny."

"Not the first time I've heard that." Holden's stare wandered over her, hovering a bit too long on her breasts before continuing down.

"Are you done?"

He had the nerve to look confused at that. "With what?"

"Never mind."

"Okay. You stay here."

"I don't even know where here is."

He hitched his head in the direction of the hood of her car. "I'd tell you to watch some television, but you drove over it."

She had bigger problems at the moment and sure hoped he had insurance. "How will you find the Congressman?"

"He'll be the one on the ground."

Holden might not be a physical threat, but

he sure was a smart-mouth. At the moment, she wasn't a fan of the personality trait. "I mean in all that space out there. You must have five acres of nothing but woods."

"More than that but not all of it's mine."

"Are you purposely misunderstanding me?"

He shot her his second smile. "Yes."

"Why?"

"I'll be right back." He made it to the gaping hole that used to be his door before he turned around again. "Forget that. I was right the first time. You're coming along."

She could barely stand up and he wanted her to run around in the dark. She was smart enough to know that wasn't a great idea. "Because?"

"I don't trust you behind me."

"You're the one with the gun."

"Which is why I'm making the rules."

Chapter Four

Holden thought about turning on the flood-lights. He had rigged the setup in the yard for an occasion just like this. He could outline every corner of his property and start a real search, but he decided against it.

Something was very wrong here, and not just the idea that he might have a dead Congressman on the premises. The problem was the identity of the possible deceased.

What were the odds the guy Holden secretly had been investigating would mistakenly find his way here, to the outskirts of Fredericks-burg, Virginia, fifty miles and a world away from the hustle of Washington, D.C.? To a place Holden lived but most people mistook for the wooded back half of a huge horse farm. The answer: not good.

"Can we walk slower?" Mia asked.

He glanced over at her. She tried to hide a

slight limp, but he picked up on it. Or, he had now that she complained. "You okay?"

"A bit sore from being slammed into the dashboard."

"Not to point out the obvious, but it wouldn't have happened if you had an air bag."

"It was stolen."

"Tonight?"

"About a month ago. Outside my apartment." She grumbled something about rotten thieves. "I parked under a streetlight and still."

"Where the hell do you live?"

"Southwest D.C."

"I hate the city." With the Recovery Project office downtown closed pending the congressional hearings, he had no reason to go to D.C. He hadn't been to the one-bedroom apartment he kept near the office for emergencies in weeks. He didn't have any plans to visit it now either.

"It's downright creepy out here," she said.

A city girl. "You get used to it."

"Everything looks the same." She stopped and turned around in a circle.

"That sort of thing happens in the woods." This time she didn't grab her head or look ready to throw up. He guessed the adrenaline had kicked in and masked the pain. Either that or this woman could fake her way through any situation. The latter option had him on edge and ready to take her down if necessary.

"How do you know which direction I drove in from?" she asked.

He pointed at the ground. "Following the tire tracks. While we're on that subject, did you even try hitting the brakes before you crashed into my house?"

"I wasn't exactly thinking straight, what with killing my boss and all."

"I guess that's fair."

As they walked, he glanced at the tall trees blocking his view of the sky. Her tires had kicked up dirt and spread gravel and leaves everywhere. "I'm not seeing anything out here except for the landscaping you mowed down."

"Does that mean you don't believe me?"

"Oh, I know you hit something."

"Is this a trust issue or do you have some superpowers I need to know about?"

Gone were the initial dazed look and slurred words. The more air she got, the more sarcastic she became. For some reason, he liked this version better.

"I saw the blood on your fender," he said.

"I have a theory."

The jump in the conversation threw him for a second but he didn't let on. "About?"

"You're not rushing to call the police because you *are* the police." She looked pleased with her theory.

"Wrong guess."

"You're law enforcement of some type."

Was. Looked as if those days were over. "How did you get there?"

"It's an educated assumption."

"Well, it's wrong because I'm actually unemployed."

She pushed branches out of her way as she walked. "I find that hard to believe."

"Why?"

"Other than the fact you don't look like the lounge-around-doing-nothing type, I have no idea."

Holden was about to shoot back an inappropriate comment about what he liked to do in his spare time when a flash of light to the far right caught his attention. The beam cut through the black distance and moved closer. Scanning the wide arc in front of him, he saw two more. Three people closing in fast.

He grabbed her arm and stopped her from taking another step. "Wait."

A twig snapped under her shoe. "What?"

"Quiet." When she started to protest, he whispered the necessary information in a rush. "We have company."

She bent her knees and hunkered down as if trying to hide from anyone who could be watching. "Walters?"

"I don't think so. No."

Not police either. Holden didn't see any of the telltale signs. No sirens. No flashing lights from a cop car. Not even any noise.

This wasn't an emergency crew checking out a call about a crash. These were the small, green, focused lights of a search party. A deadly quiet group looking for something. Holden guessed the "something" was Mia.

She shook her head. "I don't see—"

"We're going back to the house."

"It's not exactly a great hideout."

"Yeah, it is." It was the perfect place. He'd built it that way. Every member of the Recovery Project had an escape plan. He never thought he'd need one, not way out here, but it paid to be prepared. "Come on."

He took her hand. The last thing he needed was to lose her in the trees. The growth was too thick and the night too dark to take the risk.

Having one arm under his control also meant it would be harder for her to come at him if it turned out she wasn't the innocent victim she claimed to be. He hadn't performed a true search of her body for weapons, but from his visual tour he didn't see any bumps in her clothing or pockets of concern. But now that they had company, he planned on being a bit more careful.

Crouched down and kicking at a near run, they headed back to the house. As they rounded the back of the battered car, he looked over his shoulder. Mia's cheeks puffed in and out and her focus stayed on the ground. He guessed she was trying not to fall. Not a bad plan, in his view. It was the scene behind her that had him twitching.

Those lights kept moving, steady and calm, forming a perimeter and pushing in. They, whoever "they" were, descended on the house like pros. The military precision had him thinking Special Forces, but the "why" still eluded him.

Holden knew this might be about him and not Mia. He'd been digging around in private places and that sort of thing tended to make powerful people angry.

They passed through the ripped drywall,

stepping over the debris with as little crunch as possible. Without the ability to bar the door, he had limited time to get everything in order. Before she could check behind them, he guided her through the family room and down the short hall.

On the way, he grabbed his satellite phone and telescopic sight and ignored everything else. "This way."

"We can call the police," she said in a breathless hush as he hustled her into his stark bedroom.

"No time." He pressed his back against the wall and peeked out the window. The magnification provided by the goggles let him see the advance of the unwanted visitors.

"Of course there's—" She stared at him. "Binoculars?"

"An updated version, yes."

"Are the people close?"

Holden thought about lying to her. If she started crying or went into shaky shut-down mode, he might have to knock her out to rescue her. He didn't look forward to that possibility at all.

"Stand against the wall and no noise."

She obeyed. Waited all of three seconds

before talking again. "Do you have another gun?"

"Depends. Can you shoot?"

"How hard can it be?"

"So, that's a no."

He got a good look at the attackers now. And that's what they were. Dressed in black and loaded down with ammunition, they moved in unison through a mix of hand signals and nods. Mercenaries. No question these guys were guns for hire.

"We have to get out of here," he said.

"You have a plan?"

He nodded at the wall. "We're going through there."

She followed his gaze and frowned. "It's solid wood."

"Looks that way, doesn't it?"

"Wouldn't it be easier to sneak out the front? There's no door, but at least there's a hole and an obvious exit."

"The guys we're trying to avoid are at the front." He ducked down and crossed under the window. No need to give the attackers a clear target.

"What are—"

From the edge of the bed, he motioned to her. "Get on the ground and come toward me."

She didn't question this time and he was grateful.

With his blood pounding through his veins and her breathing echoing in his ear, he dropped to his knees and headed for the far wall. After crawling the short distance, he hit the floor a second before she did and collapsed with his back against the wood.

Panting now, her green eyes filled with fear, she looked over at him. "I don't understand why all this is happening."

To calm her, he brushed her wild hair back off her shoulder. "We'll get to that later."

"Are we going to have a later?"

"Count on it." He punched a series of numbers into the square black watch on his wrist until he heard a click and the wall behind them shifted. "Lean forward."

The partition lifted from the floor. He waited until it drew up about four feet and then rolled into the small room on the other side.

Her jaw dropped. "What are you doing?"

Before she even finished the sentence, he pulled her through the opening and slammed the wall shut behind them. He was on his feet and grabbing for his computer hard drive in the next breath.

Hands moving and mind shifting into gear, he inventoried the L-shaped desk and four shelves and grabbed a small backpack. He couldn't carry much but some items should come along if possible.

She brushed her fingers across the paneled wall. "What is this place?"

"It's called a SCIF."

Her hand dropped to her side but the confusion didn't clear from her face. "Come again?"

"The technical term is Sensitive Compartmented Information Facility," he said as he rifled through the desk drawer for a set of keys.

The area was an enclosed, windowless space in his house. In here he could review classified information. It functioned as a secure office within his sanctuary. The bedroom, closet and bathroom surrounded it. No one would check for it unless they knew it was there and started measuring square footage and found some missing.

"If you didn't look so serious I would think you were kidding," she said.

"'Fraid not." He pressed a remote and the monitor on the wall across from the hidden door switched from a blank screen to a shot of the area outside the house. Only one attacker was visible. That meant the other two were circling or already inside.

She watched him unzip an internal pocket of his backpack. "You're not police."

"I already said no to that."

"You're a spy."

"Not that either." He slipped his hard drive inside the space. It was the size of a paperback book but far more important. It held all of the information he'd been gathering on his secret side project, on the congressman Mia insisted she killed.

"Now what?"

"Time to go."

"Where?" She looked around the six-foot space. Then her eyes locked on the figure on the screen. "He's not police either."

"No." Holden spared the attacker a glance before punching in the password on his watch.

"What are you doing now?"

"Setting the timer to blow the place up and sending a signal for help to a friend."

"Right." She shot him a nervous smile but it faded a second later. "Wait, you're still serious?"

"Yeah."

Up until that point she'd held it together. She had paced a bit and rubbed her hands together a lot, but otherwise no craziness. With his admission about the planned explosion, her movements became frantic. Her hands flew around in the air and her voice squeaked.

"Holden, this is ridiculous. You know that, right? Please tell me you're not some lunatic serial-bomber type."

"Okay." He held both of her upper arms with a touch he hoped wouldn't terrorize her further.

"That is not a convincing response."

"I need you to stay calm."

"Then get us out of here."

"We'll have less than ten minutes."

Her green eyes turned glassy with fear. "Ten?"

"That means you do everything I say, when I say." He waited until she nodded. "Good."

He took her hands and pulled her tight against his body. He figured it was a testament to her fear that she didn't struggle or slap him. When he reached behind him and hit the small lever under his desk, the floor next to her feet rolled back to reveal a steel-reinforced opening and crudely constructed steps made of dirt wound down into the earth.

Good thing he believed in planning ahead for catastrophe.

"You are just full of surprises," she muttered as she stared into the hole that was just big enough to fit Holden.

"Here's another one." He handed her the light stick. "You're going first."

Chapter Five

By the third tread of the twenty-step decline, Mia regretted wearing heels of any type. The narrow passage barely fit a foot and the only railing was the dirt wall next to her shoulder. She had a death grip on that.

Mud caked under her nails and her shoulders ached from holding them stiff. The banging in her head hit orchestra levels.

But she didn't care. No way was she going to die on an underground staircase.

When she got halfway down, she glanced back up. Holden's light stick cast a warm glow at the top area, but she didn't see him.

"Holden?" If there was such a thing as a frantic whisper, she'd just mastered it.

The resulting silence sent the blood churning in her veins. There was no way she could do this alone. Heck, she didn't even know where she was or where this tunnel led. Those men outside with the big guns sure weren't going to help her.

With tiny shuffling steps, she turned around, ignoring the way her brain rattled and shifted. Careful not to topple backward, she grabbed on to the step above her and looked up. In the dim light she could see the tips of Holden's sneakers.

"What are you doing up there?"

"I'm coming." His voice sounded weak and a little breathy.

She didn't know how, but between climbing down and closing the door above him, he must have been injured. There was no other explanation and she had no choice but to ease her way back up the steps. "I'll be right up."

"No. Stay there."

She was pretty much done with the whole obeying thing. She'd let him know that if she didn't slip to her death.

Balancing her hands against the damp walls, she lifted one foot then the other, balancing her shoes sideways on each step, and made her way back up to him. She met him on the third one from the top. "What are you doing?"

His arms were outstretched with his fingers clamping onto the wall on either side of his body. His broad shoulders spanned the sides of the tunnel. One wrong twist and he could wedge his upper half against the dirt walls. If that happened, she'd have to dig him out with her bare hands.

"Keep going down." His husky tone vibrated.

"What is wrong with your voice?" She lifted her light and shined it on his face.

Sweat gathered on his forehead and his cheeks had bleached snow-white. "Nothing."

"What is it?" She recognized the look. She had enough training to diagnose trauma when it walked right in front of her.

"I'm okay."

"You're not."

"We don't have time to argue." He hesitated between each word.

"Are you claustrophobic?" She asked the question even though she knew the answer.

"Of course not."

Typical male. "Right. So, why is your escape route a tiny tube of mud if you can't stand enclosed spaces?"

"I've been working on it."

Now that she was paying attention, she saw the signs. The deep breaths and frenzied mumbling disguised as calm. This was something more than claustrophobia. Something worse.

She'd figure that out later. Right now she needed to get them down. "We'll have to practice coping techniques another time. Because we have about two minutes before your house explodes, we need to fast-forward your progress."

He blinked a few times. "How?"

"Let's go." She held out her hand.

He glared at her fingers.

"One step. Take a deep breath while you do it." She inhaled as an example. "Focus on a different place in your mind. A place that gives you pleasure."

He shook his head. "You need to turn around and go down."

"*We* need to move. Both of us." She wiggled her fingers at him. "Visualize that image."

After two failed tries, he pulled one hand away from the wall. Shaky and slow, he reached out to her. His palm was ice-cold.

"There you go." She wanted to give him a few minutes to get comfortable, but they didn't have time. With a gentle tug, she eased him down one step. As she walked sideways with one hand planted against the wall and the light stick between her teeth, she brought him with her.

She battled gravity and panic and the pull of his weight against her body each time she tried to lower him a step. In her head she counted down the seconds to the fireball.

"Keep breathing," she said over a mouthful of plastic.

"I am." Still unsteady but gaining speed, he moved down.

She switched the light to the hand against the mud, trapping it against the wall each time she pressed for balance. "Are you thinking about that image?"

"Yes."

"What is it?"

He was almost at the normal speed of an eighty-year-old with a walker now. "You don't want to know."

"Sure I do." Anything to keep him talking and not thinking about the walls closing in.

"Sure?"

She checked their path. Two steps from the bottom. They were almost clear. "Yep."

"You…"

"That's nice."

"Naked."

Her foot slipped but his vise grip and a

hasty grab for the wall saved her from sliding down the rest of the way on her face. Pebbles tumbled and her light stick went flying. She landed in a sprawl with one hand stretched out in front of her, holding his.

Sitting on a stair with her pride squashed under her, she glanced up at him. "Was that necessary?"

Through the sweating and the slight tremble of his arm, he smiled. "You asked."

"Yeah, well. I'm sorry I did." She kicked out her legs and hit the bottom. Being less than gentle, she tugged him down after. "Keep your mind on the rescue."

"Yes, ma'am."

She dropped his hand and wiped her palms against her pants. Locating the light stick took longer. It had rolled under a rock crevice. Despite pulling on it, the thing wouldn't budge.

She gave up and stood. "Now what?"

The words barely escaped her mouth when the ground shook. One minute she stared into the bleak darkness of the tunnel ahead and the next her feet left the floor.

Strong arms wrapped around her waist. Holden's shout vibrated in her head as he dragged her to the ground. She saw the mud coming up to greet her and couldn't put out her hands to break the fall. He had trapped them at her sides.

At the last second, he shifted his weight and took the brunt of their combined weight on his shoulder. A rough breath blew against her cheek right before he pressed his hand to the back of her neck and tucked her head under his chin as he rolled on top of her.

Beneath her, the ground shifted from side to side. Above her, a mix of shattering booms and Holden's harsh breathing filled her ears. She waited for the ceiling to cave in as mud and chunks of rock fell all around them. None of it touched her, but she could feel Holden take the impact and groan each time he got hit.

An odd roar rumbled through the tunnel. "What is that?"

"The fire." He finally looked at her. "You okay?"

"No, but I can move."

"Good." He eased off of her. "We're going to run."

"Are you worried about a cave-in?

"I'm worried I won't be able to get out of here otherwise. It's getting tighter every second." He leaped to his feet.

She saw a rip in his backpack and blood

running down his arm. But it was the frantic look in his blue eyes that told her what she needed to know. Being inside this mud tube was killing him.

"Let's go," she agreed.

With her hand in his and only his light as a guide, they raced down the long hall. Something scurried ahead of them but she ignored it. Every creature for itself.

Twenty feet after a sharp turn, they hit a wall. "Holden!"

"We're fine." Another touch of his watch and the dirt wall slid open. "The other side is steel."

"You'll have to tell me why an unemployed non-spy has this setup."

"Once we're safe." He dug his fingers into the small opening and pushed a door no one but him could see a second ago.

A sudden rush of cold air smacked her in the face, sending a shiver spinning through her. Walking from one dank, dark place into the black openness of the woods didn't do anything for her vision. She couldn't see anything except the towering trees surrounding them on three sides and the orange flame licking into the sky behind them.

The fire crackled and danced, jumping from

the burning heap of the former cabin to the branches of the nearby trees. Without help, this could spread and cause a disaster.

Holden closed the door and then leaned against it. The seam blended into the landscape until only the rock at the base of a small hill was visible. He, however, still had the green tint around his mouth. Even without any decent light she could see that.

"You okay?" She rubbed a hand up and down his arm as she asked.

"Fine." He inhaled nice and deep. The air seemed to revive him. "We're not out of the woods yet."

"Literally."

"We need to keep moving, just in case one of those guys got out in time." Holden delivered the insight with his commanding tone back in place. Then he started walking.

Not wanting to be left behind, she took off after him and reached for his wrist. "Where are we going?"

"To the truck."

Maybe he hit his head. "Do you see a truck?"

He leaned his mouth down close to her ear. "Trust me."

Another few steps and they ran into a pile

of branches she hadn't seen the minute before. He dumped his pack on the ground and wasted no time throwing the limbs on a stack to the side. Slowly, he uncovered a beat-up pickup truck. It was small, possibly once was green and didn't look as if it could go a mile without chugging to a stop.

"Really?" she asked.

"Get in."

It took five pulls before the door opened. When it did, it flew out of her hands, creaking as it went. She ignored his glare and every pain in her body as she hopped inside.

"Not the quietest getaway ever." Mumbling under his breath, he chucked his pack on the floor.

He turned the key and kept the lights off. Remarkably, the engine started. It didn't clink or sputter either.

With the truck in Reverse, he rested his arm across the back of the bench seat. Whatever he was about to say had him grinning, but then his mouth fell into a flat line. "Get down!"

She didn't think. Hands over her head, she ducked but not before she saw the beam of green light flash across the front of the car.

Holden yanked the wheel hard to the left as

he stepped on the gas. His grip didn't ease as he bent down, bringing his head close to hers.

"Go faster!" She screamed the command with all the out-of-control terror bubbling inside her.

"Can't." He pressed her farther into the seat with his free hand. "We'll get stuck in the mud."

She could feel the energy pounding off him as pinging sounds echoed all around her. The tires slid and the back of the car moved as if separate from the front. With a sudden crack, the window next to her head shattered and the car slowed.

She lost all ability to talk, to do anything, when a hand draped in a black glove reached into the truck. It slapped for her, grabbing for her hair, but she pressed her body low against the seat and begged Holden to do something.

She watched him morph into superspy mode. With one hand on the wheel and his foot on the gas, he threw out his free arm and pointed his gun at the darkness over her shoulder.

The deafening blast exploded right next to her face. She saw a burst of light and heard the thundering boom. Then the offensive hand fell away.

By the time she sat up, Holden had maneuvered them out of whatever had a hold of the wheel. They spun around in a circle and drove about five feet before he slowed to a stop.

"What are you doing?" she asked, her voice rubbed raw from all the yelling and panic.

"Checking." He was out of the truck before she could stop him.

She slid across the seat and peeked out the driver's side door. "Holden!"

"Do not move," he called back.

Her muscles were frozen. If she wanted to jump down, run—anything—she couldn't. She hadn't realized she was holding her breath until he ran back and slid into his seat.

She smacked his arm.

"Hey!" He had the nerve to look offended.

"What were you thinking?"

"That I could identify him."

Her breath caught in her throat. "Did you?"

"No." Holden kept glancing in his rearview mirror as he drove slow but steady through the chocking woods.

"Is he…"

"Dead?" Holden looked at her then. The

terrified anguish from the tunnel was gone. He wore a mask of fury now.

She didn't know if he was angry with her or coasting on adrenaline. Either way, she didn't appreciate the barking. If he wanted attitude, she was more than prepared to show him some.

"Well, is he?"

"Very."

Chapter Six

In the past hour he'd shot a man through the forehead and crawled through a tunnel. Only one of those things made Holden want to throw up. The fact that the small space scared him more than the killing made his stomach churn and heave even more.

Four years out of the military—away from the night that haunted him, breaking into his sleep at least once a week—and tight spaces still dropped him to his knees. And this time he had a witness.

No one, not even his fellow Recovery agents, knew about his private fears. Now Mia did. That fact ticked him off. It was the sort of weapon he didn't hand anyone.

They walked down the hall of the nondescript condo building, his anger festering with every step. A part of him knew picking her out as the target of his rage and frustration was irrational. The other part of him didn't care.

She broke into his sanctuary and dragged him out of it. Because of her, he lost his house and everything in it. He wasn't one to collect stuff. He learned the hard way to travel light, but whenever he'd left before the choice had been his. This time, he got his butt kicked out by a hot blonde and a raging fire. He didn't know which of these he liked less. The mix of the two sure as heck wasn't his favorite.

"Do you want to talk about it?" she asked.

He stopped in front of Rod's door and rang the bell. "No."

"There are therapies—"

Holden's hand hesitated over the doorknob. "Don't."

"They could help."

He faced her. "I'm sure you know what 'don't' means."

"Are you always this testy?"

Something about her getting angry sucked the fight right out of him. He hoped he hadn't gotten to the point where bossy women turned him on. If so, he might try that therapy after all.

"Being chased and shot at does that to me," he said. "Yeah."

"That's not what I was talking about."

He knew that. Knew it and ignored it. The claustrophobia was not up for discussion. Ever.

When the doorknob twisting and knocking didn't work, Holden dug the key chain out of his pocket. "We'll do it this way."

She glanced down both ends of the hall. "Is this your place?"

"Belongs to my boss."

"I thought you were unemployed."

"Former boss, then."

"I get the sneaky suspicion there's a part of this story I'm missing."

"That's what I like about smart women."

"What?" she asked.

"Almost everything, actually." She snorted and he almost joined her. "For the record, it surprises me, too."

He pushed the door open and motioned for her to stay back while he walked inside. A quick look around told Holden what he needed to know. Rod wasn't there. He would have greeted them with a gun if he had been.

No one came into Rod Lehman's place without an invitation. It didn't matter that all of the Recovery agents had keys to each other's places or that Holden called first. Rod was a "threaten first, ask questions later" kind of guy.

"Your friend is very…neat," she said as she touched the perfectly straight stack of magazines.

Holden knew better. Rod set up the place whenever he left. Everything in its place so that he'd know if anyone came in while he was gone. Then there was the fact this wasn't Rod's true home.

Like Holden, Rod lived outside D.C. Rod's choice was a farm in a tiny town in Maryland, near the West Virginia border. Here in the city he had a one-bedroom with beige walls and minimal furniture in a drab shade of brown. It was small enough to see every corner no matter where you stood. There he had two acres and a security system that rivaled the one at NORAD.

Holden headed for the kitchen lining the far left wall. He opened the refrigerator and saw barren shelves that went beyond a bachelor's stark existence.

"Hungry?" she asked in a voice filled with sarcasm.

"Just checking." Holden took a quick look around. Despite the empty place, something felt off. The muscle at the base of his neck began to throb. That was never a good sign. "Stay here."

She saluted him. "Yes, sir."

He stopped right in front of her. "Is that your way of saying I'm demanding?"

She moved her finger and thumb almost together. "Little bit."

Being this close to her, he noticed the cuts on her face and the smudge of mud on her cheek. Under all that dirt lurked a stunning woman. Big eyes and a sassy mouth. It was a killer combination that kicked his lust into high gear.

"You do understand that you came driving into my family room, right?"

"I'm sorry about that." She had the decency to wince.

"You're sorry?"

The brief window of guilt zapped closed. Her mouth curled down in a frown. "I can barely stand, my skull feels like it's about to break open and I'm pretty sure I have someone else's blood in my hair."

He fought back a smile. "And?"

"Then there's the part where someone is trying to kill me and I have no idea why. So, I'm sorry if you find me unpleasant or ungrateful, but I just don't have it in me at the moment to care."

Spunk. He didn't want to, but he liked it. "Fair enough."

She was the first one to look away. She waved him toward the room on the other side of the condo. "Check the bedroom. I'm going to wash my hands."

"The sink is right there."

She rolled her eyes at him. "I can still see."

"And talk. You haven't lost that skill either."

She ran her hand under the water, letting the warmth run through her. Grabbing for a towel, she went in search of an aspirin to stop her head from exploding. She pulled open the thin door next to the refrigerator thinking to find a pantry.

A man stood there, all curled up and impossibly tight in the small space. More than his position, she noticed the knife in his hand. The blade had to be five inches long.

The stranger pressed a finger to his lips. "Quiet."

No freaking way.

She turned to run, thinking to put as much space between her and the sharp edge as possible and it gave her a few extra seconds to scream for Holden. For anyone with a gun within screaming range, actually.

Holden emerged from the bedroom at a sprint right as their mystery guest hooked his elbow around her throat. The edge of the knife pricked her neck.

She flinched at the contact and got nipped again. To keep the weapon as far away as possible, she grabbed on to the arm of her attacker and pushed.

Holden's gaze flicked to the trickle of blood she could feel running down her neck and back to the man behind her. "Let's calm down here," Holden said.

"I'm in charge." The attacker's hot creepy breath skipped across her skin.

Fear replaced her headache. Her insides trembled as her knees lost their strength. She thought about elbowing the guy in the stomach or dropping to the floor and out of his reach—doing anything before she lost the ability to fight—but something in Holden's cold stare told her to stay put.

"There's no reason to hurt her," he said.

The guy's grip tightened on her throat. "Where is it?"

Confusion flashed across Holden's face but

he quickly controlled it. "Tell me what you want. I'm sure we can work this out."

She knew Holden had a gun behind his back. She guessed he had other weapons, too. He seemed like the kind of guy who was prepared for an attack. At least she hoped that was true.

"Give it to me." The attacker waved the knife in front of her face.

"What is it?" Holden's gaze made a quick tour of the room.

She doubted her attacker even saw the move. He was too busy spitting in her hair while he choked the life out of her.

"Don't play dumb," the man said, pulling on her neck until the bones crunched.

Holden nodded as his feet shuffled slightly. "You're right. I have it. It's in my car."

What? She stared at Holden, trying to figure out if he was playing along or risking her life. She wasn't thrilled with either option because she feared they both ended up the same—with her bleeding to death on the floor.

The stranglehold on her windpipe eased. "Where?"

"Just downstairs in the garage." Holden pressed down with his hand as if trying to calm the situation. "There's no reason to panic. We'll go down and—"

"No." The attacker shifted positions. "And stop moving."

Holden's eyebrow lifted but he stayed quiet. As if he hadn't heard the command, he kept his feet in motion. Small steps, tiny really, with just enough of a turn to put his back toward the front door and the attacker's toward the window.

She had no idea what Holden had planned. They were on the fifth floor. Unless he intended to push the guy out or scale up the side later to rescue her, the movements didn't make sense.

"You have two minutes."

Holden lowered his hand. "For what?"

"You go down and get it, and I'll wait here with your girlfriend."

Holden was already shaking his head. "I'm not leaving her."

Relief flooded through her. Whatever was about to happen, she wouldn't have to face it alone.

"Then she's dead," the attacker said in a tone that suggested he welcomed the idea.

- "There's got to be another way," Holden said.

"You go and I'll take care of her." The attacker's hand slipped down her silk shirt to right above her breast.

She tried to push his fingers away but the knife edged her ear. "Holden, do something."

The attacker's hand hesitated. "I thought your name was Rod."

Holden kept his focus locked on the other man. "It is. She's using a nickname."

"You go get it and I'd move fast because I'm going to be touching your girl while you're gone." His palm settled over her breast, roughly cupping her.

Bile rushed up her throat. The idea of the man's hands roaming over her brought her fight-or-flight instincts racing back to life. She swallowed hard to keep control. The knife was too close and letting this guy know he scared her would only bring him pleasure.

Holden took a step closer. He didn't try to hide this one. "We'll both go down."

"Your two minutes have started." The attacker put his mouth on the side of her face and inhaled. "She's going to be good."

"Don't touch her."

"I'll be touching her, all right." His fingers

tightened over her breast. "So I'd move if I were you."

"Right." Holden looked at her then.

Those blue eyes were willing her to do something. She just didn't know what. She concentrated on him, blocking out the man twisting his body around hers.

Holden's quick glance down at his hand happened so fast she almost missed it. One finger. Two. A countdown to something. When he showed three, she pushed all her weight away from the knife's edge.

The brief diversion threw her attacker off balance. "You bitch!"

The last half of the word gurgled out of him as he dropped the weapon and grabbed for his neck with both hands. Blood spurted as he gagged. Losing control of his legs, he slipped to the floor and fell back against the hardwood.

The whole scene took only seconds, but she watched it in slow motion. She lost all feeling in her fingers and the air pumping through her made her lungs ache.

It wasn't until she glanced over at Holden that she realized what had happened. He stood with his arm still extended from where he threw the knife.

Then he was at her side. "Mia?"

"I don't—"

He cradled her to his chest. "It's okay. We're going to get you out of here."

"Who was he?" she mumbled the question in Holden's shirt.

"I don't know, but you're safe now."

She was because Holden had killed for her.

Again.

Chapter Seven

Luke Hathaway opened the door as Holden and Mia hit the front porch. Holden hated to drag this mess into his friend's home. Even with a messed-up arm, Luke could take just about anything anyone threw at him. But still.

Luke and his new wife, Claire, lived in suburban Maryland, just outside of D.C., in a deceptively modest house surrounded by tall trees and a fence with metal tips sharp enough to puncture anyone who dared try to climb it.

The area was home to horse farms and mansions owned by lobbyists and partners at downtown law firms. And congressmen. Walters lived four blocks away. Holden knew because he made it his business to know everything about Walters, the congressman heading up the top-secret hearings about the Recovery Project and its leader, Rod Lehman.

The only thing Holden wasn't clear on at the moment was whether or not the Congressman was alive.

"Sorry to drop in on you," Holden said.

"Damn, you look like hell," Luke joked until his attention moved to Mia and a killing rage washed over his face. "What happened to you?"

She touched her hair and then glared at Holden. "Is it bad?"

"You're fine." He worried that wasn't really the case. Adrenaline kept her moving, but an inevitable crash hovered on the horizon. He could tell from the growing daze in her eyes and the way she touched her head every few seconds, as if that would stop the headache budding inside.

Mia combed fingers through her hair in a nervous gesture he found oddly endearing. "You should tell a person when she looks scary."

He shrugged, pretending all was well. No need to get her riled up. Glancing in a mirror would do that without any help from him. "Luke's seen worse."

"Do I really look that bad?" she asked Luke.

"Honestly? You don't look good."

"Luke!" Claire Hathaway pushed her husband out of the way and motioned her visitors inside.

Dark hair and sexy as hell. Holden had liked Claire on sight and not just for that curvy body, though that was bonus. She was the one woman capable of handling a man like Luke. She had stormed back into his life after a broken engagement and taken over. He was still a perfect shot and tough as hell, but Claire grounded him. Gave him focus and a sense of purpose.

But it hadn't come easy. Luke and Claire shared a complicated history. She'd been subjected to more than her share of gossip, still was, but her love for Luke had never been in question. At least not by Holden. He noticed it right off. It took Luke a bit longer to wake up and see it.

They all stepped inside the cozy craftsman-style home and stopped in the entryway at the bottom of the stairs. To the right was a formal dining room that was doing double duty as an office. On the left, a family room. A fire burned in the fireplace and two puffy couches faced each other in front of it.

Because Luke kept glancing at Mia with a frown of concern that grew more severe with each peek, Holden skipped to the introductions. "Luke and Claire Hathaway, this is Mia Landers."

Claire's smile faltered as she looked at Mia. "What did Holden do to you?"

Mia leaned closer to Holden. "Saved my life."

"Twice," he said. Her protective shift pleased him to a ridiculous degree. He cleared his throat to keep from letting it show. "For the record."

"Show-off," Luke mumbled under his breath, then threw his wife a "what did I say?" look when she stared him down. "We got the alarm code. Adam, Caleb and Zach are on the way to see if they can help."

"Who are they?" Mia asked.

Luke maneuvered the group to the couches in the family room as Claire slipped into the kitchen at the back of the house. "We all work together."

"Holden said he was unemployed."

Claire retuned with a tray filled with mugs and a coffeepot. "Technically, he's not wrong."

Luke waited until Claire set the items on the table before pouring Mia a cup of black coffee and handing it to her. "What happened?"

Holden took that one. "My house exploded."

Mia closed her eyes as she took a sip of the steaming liquid. "And I killed Representative Walters."

Luke dropped his cup but pulled off an impressive deep-knee bend to grab it before it crashed against the polished hardwood floor. "Excuse me?"

Claire hadn't stopped watching Mia. "Is that blood on your shirt?"

Mia didn't bother to look down. "And mud and who knows what else. I'm trying not to think about it."

Holden winced at the list. "The blood's not hers."

"Yeah, Holden, that makes it better." Claire took the mug out of Mia's hands. "We should get you cleaned up."

Mia didn't move. "Why do you look familiar?"

Holden figured Mia had dealt with enough this evening. Hearing about Claire's past would only wind them all up again. "Now isn't the best time for that."

Claire waved off the concern. "It's okay."

"What?" Mia asked as she looked around at the other faces in the room.

"You probably saw my photo all over the news as Claire Samson."

"I hate that last name." Luke rubbed his shoulder as he said it.

"No arguments here." Holden could still remember the scene. Luke on the ground bleeding and Claire being dragged away to prison for a murder she didn't commit. The road from there to their happy-ever-after had not been an easy one.

"I was accused of killing my ex-husband, Phil."

Mia visibly inhaled. "Oh."

"Sound familiar?" Holden asked even though he knew the answer. Everyone knew the story. Phil was dead and his brother, Steve, was in prison awaiting trial on a host of fraud and securities charges in addition to those for murder and attempted murder. The fallout took down the Recovery Project, a previously top-secret organization, and its leader.

Mia faced Luke, then her gaze skipped to Holden. "You're part of the group the Congressman is holding the hearings about."

"He didn't like that we were out there operating undercover and he didn't know about us or have control over our funding." Luke ticked off their supposed sins on his fingers.

Holden saw a bigger hole. "How do you know about the Recovery Project? Our existence is need-to-know only and the hearings are supposed to be hush-hush."

"Everyone in the office knows. The Congressman is determined to make sure none of you work in law enforcement again." Mia winced. "Sorry."

The sentiment wasn't a surprise, but it still ticked off Holden. Walters had all but promised to destroy Rod Lehman. Walters had been too close with the Samson brothers to not exact revenge. Same clubs, same schools, same old-moneyed backgrounds.

"Guess that confirms our fear that the Project will never get back on track," Holden said.

"And that's enough for Mia." Claire clapped to get everyone's attention. "Whatever you need to talk about can wait ten minutes while she gets a shower."

"I'm fine." Mia's halfhearted attempt to call Claire off didn't work, which was inevitable because Claire wasn't one to be put off.

She wrapped an arm around Mia's slim shoulders and guided her toward the stairs. The entire time she glared at Holden. "We'll talk about this later."

Nothing like having two women angry with him. "Don't blame me."

The comment fell flat because Claire already had Mia on the bottom step. "You're probably a size smaller than me, but we can find some sweats that will work."

"I don't think—"

Claire called over her shoulder to the men. "We'll be right back."

Luke held his blank look until the women's legs disappeared at the top of the stairs, then his venom unleashed. "Walters is dead?"

"Mia seems to think so." Holden started to sit down and then thought better of it. Caked with mud, he fit in at his home. Not here. If he messed up the couch, Claire might strangle him.

"Why?"

"Mia says she ran him over with her car." When Luke tried to say something, Holden cut him off. "I can explain the whole thing, including a few dead guys we'll need to handle."

"We?"

"But I need a favor first."

Luke dropped onto his couch and nodded to the one across from him for Holden to do the same. "Name it."

That's one of the things Holden admired

about Luke. He didn't fluster. You handed him a problem and he resolved it. He slid right into leadership mode and took over.

"Do a background check on Mia," Holden said, knowing the idea would rile Luke. He had a soft spot for the ladies, especially petite, pretty ones like Mia.

"Not without an explanation."

Holden balanced on the very edge of the sofa. "She says she works for Walters, but I haven't heard of her."

"Not unusual if she's a worker bee."

"She's got this story about how Walters had her drive out to the woods near my place before he went nuts and then attacked her."

Luke's eyebrows snapped together. "What the hell?"

"Exactly."

"Walters is a lot of things, but a rapist?"

Rape. Holden's brain traveled back to Rod's condo and that man's hand on Mia's breast. The helpless anguish on her face. The disgust that churned in his gut as his mind jumped right to murderous rage. Letting the attacker touch her for even two seconds had chipped away at Holden's humanity. Forget getting the guy off of her, Holden had wanted him dead.

"We might need a doctor." Claire's voice broke into the darkness swirling around him. The shaky thread to her tone had both men standing.

Holden knew worry when he saw it. "Is Mia okay?"

"She's crashing on me." Claire glanced back at the staircase, then lowered her voice to a whisper. "I'm assuming her energy just ran out, but her eyes are glassy. Like she has a concussion or something."

Holden feared that might be the case. That or shock. If she truly was a Capitol Hill worker, then having men drop dead at her feet and getting pawed by some creature would not be a regular occurrence.

"Did she hit her head?" Claire asked.

"Probably. I mean, she drove her car through my front door."

Luke and Claire just stared, mouths open and wearing identical what-the-hell frowns. Neither said a word.

"What?" Holden asked.

"You left out that piece of information earlier. It's kind of important." Luke didn't try to hide his exasperation until he turned to Claire and his voice lowered to a more reasonable decibel. "Caleb should be here any minute."

"In the meantime, she needs help in the bathroom." Claire's tone suggested she expected Holden to take over and now.

"Why are you looking at me?" he asked.

"I thought she might be more comfortable undressing with you than a complete stranger."

Mia. Naked. No, that was never going to work. She needed medical care, not him drooling over her. "I've known her for three hours."

"So?"

Holden was wondering if Claire meant to drive him insane. "Not sexually."

"Oh." Then Claire's face changed. "Ohhhhh."

"I've never seen her without clothes, haven't even kissed her yet." Holden tried to snatch the last word back but it was too late. It was out there, just bumping around.

And Luke noticed. He covered his mouth with his hand even though it did nothing to hide his smile. "Apparently you're slipping."

Claire rolled her eyes at both of them. "Fine. You stay here. I'll handle this."

It took another fifteen minutes for everyone to show up. Looking around Luke's dining-room table, Holden felt nothing but gratitude.

He had sent up a virtual flare and they all came running.

Adam Wright sat down, opened his ever-present laptop and started typing before anyone said a word. Caleb Mattern stood there with his medical bag, shifting from foot to foot, clearly wanting to get upstairs to his patient. And Zach Bachman, Zach being Zach and a demolitions expert, smelled like sulfur. Holden had enough problems so he didn't ask.

Ever since the congressional hearings started, they'd scattered to their realms of privacy and seen each other less frequently. It wasn't until they met again that Holden realized how much he missed the daily interaction. Finding missing people meant they didn't hang out in the office much, but they did confer. Not working meant not having that intellectual stimulation, but that dry spell was over now.

Holden ran through the Mia scenario with the team. Luke fired questions about the car, the men who stormed the house and the two Holden killed. The others just listened.

Then the conversation stopped. Holden sat with his back to the entry, so he wasn't exactly sure what happened until he smelled flowers and heard the shuffle of feet. No question Mia had joined them.

He turned around, intending to make a comment but the joke, whatever it was, died on his lips. She wore a slim gray T-shirt and sloppy black sweats that stopped at her knees. The outfit should have said comfort. To Holden it said smoking hot. Clean with shiny blond hair and rosy cheeks, she hardly resembled the woman who dragged him to safety through an underground tunnel while wearing a proper business suit. This Mia looked soft and pretty and a bit too irresistible for his liking.

Apparently he wasn't alone because Caleb practically fell out of his chair when she crossed the threshold. Adam even stopped typing. Zach did a double take, which was about as much interest as he ever showed in anything.

Claire walked into the room with her head down and almost slammed into Mia. She glanced around the room, looking less happy the longer she went. "What's wrong with you all?"

Holden knew the answer to that one. "A case of male idiocy."

"You guys have seen a woman before, right?" Claire put her hand on Mia's back and shifted until she stood slightly in front of her.

Luke's eyebrow lifted. "You're one."

"They don't think of me as a woman."

Adam snorted, then scooted his chair back when Luke swung an arm in his direction.

Holden decided to take over. It was either that or tick Claire off further, and no smart man would pick that option. He did a quick round of introductions, then pulled out a chair for Mia.

"I'm not sure you should be out of bed," Caleb said.

"My head hurts if I'm sitting up or lying down, so I figured I'd say hello." Mia pointed at Holden's coffee mug. "May I?"

She didn't wait for permission and he didn't stop her. He was too busy looming over her and watching for signs of trauma. If she passed out he'd have his answer, but he hoped it wouldn't come to that. Her color seemed too bright and her eyes more watery than focused.

"The pain thing kind of proves my point." Caleb shot her a smile that had her smiling right back.

Holden tightened his grip on the back of the chair. "That's enough of that."

Mia turned around and looked up at him. "What's wrong?"

"Interesting," Luke said at the same time.

Holden refused to acknowledge the wave of jealousy that smacked him. He wasn't about to let his buddies do it either.

He dropped down in the chair next to hers. "Nothing."

"I'm sorry I dragged all of you into my mess." Mia glanced around the table, then reached out her hand to cover Holden's. "Especially you. When I think about your house…"

"That wasn't your fault."

She squeezed his fingers. "And then I made you go down that staircase when you couldn't breathe."

Holden felt a thud against his rib cage. "Mia—"

"Why couldn't you breathe?" Adam asked.

"The claustrophobia." She spit out the answer before Holden could stop her.

He closed his eyes, hoping no one heard. When he opened them again he knew—no such luck. They were all looking at him.

Luke tapped on the table to get Mia's attention. "What?"

"The small spaces…" She stopped gesturing with her hands. "Wait, you all didn't know?"

Holden blew out a shaky breath. "They do now."

"Since when have you had this issue?" Caleb asked.

Zach was the one who answered. "Doesn't matter. Let's move on."

Holden appreciated the assist. Zach knew exactly what happened and when. He was there. He lived it, or part of it. Somehow he moved past it. Holden hadn't figured out how to do the same.

The sadness on Mia's face deepened. "My point is that I brought all of this danger to you. Me and my boss."

"About that." Holden refused to talk about the demons that taunted him, but he needed to come clean about this. "It wasn't exactly your fault that you ended up at my house."

"I drove through it."

"Well, that was all you. Thanks again, but I'm talking about the circumstances that put you in the woods near my house."

Mia eyes narrowed. "What do you mean?"

Holden leaned forward on his elbow and tried to block out the unwanted audience. "It was me."

"What was?"

"I hacked into Walters's computer."

Luke slammed his hand against the table. "Damn it, Holden."

"Why?" Mia glanced around the table as if looking for support or an explanation. "I don't get it."

"Your boss is—or was—investigating our team and the work we used to do."

Adam stopped tapping on his computer keys. "Why didn't you ask me to do it?"

"Adam." Luke's warning rang through the otherwise-quiet room.

"I'm the security expert." Adam pointed at his laptop as if to prove his point.

Mia tightened her hand, bringing Holden's attention back to her. "I still don't under-stand."

He glanced down, letting the guilt fill him. He deserved the hollow feeling in his stom-ach. He knew that. "I used what I thought was an empty user file and bounced the signal, thinking Walters or his people wouldn't be able to track it down."

Shock registered on Mia's mouth right before she pulled her hand away from him. "You set me up?"

"Not on purpose."

The exhaustion tugging at her mouth disappeared in a flash. Her cheeks blushed bright pink. "The Congressman was convinced I was working with someone."

"He figured out I was in. He just didn't know that I got there without any help."

She stood up fast enough to knock over her chair and had to grab on to the edge of the table to keep from falling. "He attacked me, Holden."

He reached out to steady her, but she shrugged his hand away. He tried not to let the dismissal bug him. "I know."

"I had to mow the man down with my car to keep him from killing me."

"That's enough." Caleb got up, sparing Holden only a second's glare before facing Mia. "Now isn't the time for this."

"Of course it is," she insisted.

"You have plenty of stress without this conversation. I want to check your head and see what we're dealing with here. See, I'm the medical and science guy around here."

"Good idea. Let's make sure she's okay." Holden tried to get out of his seat.

Claire shoved him back down with much more force than was necessary. "You stay. Seems you have some explaining to do."

Luke barely waited until Caleb and Claire guided Mia from the room. "What were you thinking?"

Holden didn't pretend to misunderstand. "I wanted Walters to leave the Recovery Project alone so we could get back to work."

"Nice job," Adam said.

Holden went to take a drink, then realized Mia finished his coffee. "You're all forgetting the bigger issue."

Zach tapped his pen against the table. "There's something bigger than killing a sitting member of the U.S. House of Representatives?"

"Rod is missing and we're not one inch closer to finding him."

Adam nodded. "True."

"Someone was at his house and that someone was looking for something. We need to figure out what it was."

"Agreed, but this time we do it as a team." Luke's stare suggested they all agree.

Holden did.

Chapter Eight

Bram Walters flinched as a string of profanity escaped his lips on a hiss. If the doctor tugged the bandage any tighter, the broken ribs would poke right out of the skin.

"Take it easy," Bram said.

The doctor's nervous smile faded. "I need to give you a shot."

"No." He couldn't afford to lose any more brain power to pain meds.

"Listen to the man, Bram." Trevor Walters shoved open the door to the back room of the small medical clinic, shouting orders and texting on his phone as he walked.

It was almost three in the morning and no one was around except the people Trevor required to be there. Bram was the Congressman, but Trevor thought he ran the show. Typical older, powerful brother with a God complex. Bram ignored the ego because he needed help.

"About time you showed up." Leave it to Trevor to appear after the fighting ended. Just one more reason for Bram to question who was taking the biggest risk in this deal.

Trevor stared down the doctor. "Leave us for a minute."

Bram waited until they were alone to express his concern. "Can he be trusted?"

"The doctor is on my payroll."

"Is there anyone who isn't?" Only someone who worked for Trevor would be unimpressed with a member of Congress showing up on his doorstep in the middle of the night needing medical attention.

"Mia Landers."

"What about her?"

Trevor shoved his phone into his coat pocket. "What made you think you should handle that loose end on your own?"

"She's my employee. I was driving her out there to ask questions and flush out her partner. You didn't need to interfere."

"A poorly thought-out plan."

Trevor took a difficult situation and blew it out of control, but Bram knew his brother would never admit it. "Only because you sent the commandos after me. What were you thinking?"

"That I needed to clean up your mess. It's a good thing I had my men ready or you'd still be lying out there in the woods."

"Clearly I miscalculated about Mia, but the fire fight is your responsibility." Bram remembered bits and pieces of the night. Two armed men breaking out of the bushes and grabbing him. Flames shooting into the sky. "No one was supposed to get hurt."

"Thanks to your employee and her meddling, that was no longer an option."

The disloyal bitch. Bram couldn't think about her without wanting to tear something, or someone, apart. He hired her because of her long, sentimental speech about wanting a second career, one that would allow her to serve her country.

None of that washed with him, but it had impressed his chief of staff, David Brennan. Thinking back now, David probably thought he could make a move on Mia. And for Bram, having a pretty blonde in his office wasn't a hardship. It always paid to bring someone interesting to a committee meeting. It got attention when he needed it.

But she had deceived him, turned on him in the most disloyal way. She linked up with someone who was trying to destroy him, who dared break into his private space.

"As usual, I did the dirty work so you could keep your hands clean," Trevor said.

Bram wasn't up for a round of arguing. He also wasn't in the mood for his brother's condescending crap. "I didn't ask you to step in."

"You brought us into this situation. I'm merely trying to get you out of it."

As far as Bram was concerned, the main problem was gone. "Mia died in the fire."

"I'm not so sure."

"Meaning?"

"We're still sifting through the debris and bodies."

"Why did you cause such a scene? Now we have to explain it."

"I didn't." Trevor raised his hand to stop Bram from butting in. "The official line is gas explosion, but I think we'll find it was rigged to blow by the owner of that cabin."

"But you have the police and fire department under control."

"Of course, but that still leaves a serious issue." Trevor eyed the tray of scalpels and bandages.

"What?"

"A who, to be more precise. The partner. The man who helped Mia."

Bram felt another string unravel. Trevor's simple plan to resolve the Mia problem was turning out to be anything but. "You think it's someone tied to Lehman?"

"Of course."

"We have other enemies."

"That's true, but there's no reason for anyone else to set us up like this. We're giving our contact at the Witness Security Program everything he needs. We have an understanding. *That* is under control."

Bram wasn't convinced.

"Besides, look at the timing," Trevor said. "You shut down Lehman's group and someone hacks into your computer. Not your office computer. No, your personal files. You go after your legislative staffer for answers, and someone with serious advanced skills rushes in to rescue her."

"Give me a name."

"Can't yet. The ownership of the house is buried in legal documents and dummy companies. It will take some time to track down, but my people are working on it. We should know something in two days."

"Until then?"

"Everything points to Lehman or one of his agents."

"The group disbanded. I saw to that when I did what I had to do to have them all put on administrative leave. My sources say they peeled off and are lying low."

Trevor put down the metal instrument he was holding. "From my experience, men who work together at that level function like military operatives at war. That bond isn't easily broken."

And Trevor would know about that sort of surgical precision. He ran a lucrative operation. Companies, even governments, turned to him for logistical assistance in areas of the world where lawlessness ruled. He advised corporations about international kidnapping risks. He made enemies of terrorists and friends of people in power.

"It's time we investigated all of the former Recovery Project's members and not just Rod Lehman," Trevor said.

Bram was one step ahead this time. He planned to issue the subpoenas and bring them all in to testify under oath. "I am as part of the hearing."

"You handle that end and I'll take care of the rest."

"What else is there?" Bram asked.

"Do you really want to know?"

He didn't hesitate. "No."

MIA FELT AS IF she was suffocating. Her heart pounded and her arms flailed. She woke up with a start and realized the problem. Pushing the white fluffy comforter off her face, she balanced on her elbows and glanced around the strange room.

A bedroom and it wasn't hers. Clean-lined Shaker furniture and billowy blue curtains covering oversize windows. A light on each nightstand and a stack of pillows behind her head that nearly put her in a sitting position.

She didn't recognize anything except the sleeping man next to her. Holden wore faded jeans and a clean T-shirt. His dark hair glistened, suggesting he took time for a shower. He sure smelled better than he did in the underground tunnel. Something with a citrus tint.

She was tucked under the covers and he lay on top. She couldn't remember how either of those things happened. A quick peek under the sheet calmed her anxiety about having been stripped naked. The pants were gone, but she still wore the T-shirt.

The quiet gave her time to study Holden. He rested his back against the headboard with his arms crossed over his chest. She barely knew him, yet she trusted him. She'd put her life in his hands several times without any promise that he'd keep it safe. Yet he had.

For someone who kept her distance and held men off, it was a surprise. She'd learned the hard way that some men didn't deserve a chance. This one played a role in the predicament she now found herself. When she first heard the news, it hit her like a brick to the face. He was fooling around in a private computer and incriminated her.

But no matter how hard she tried, she couldn't hold on to her anger. Holden hadn't targeted her. He'd gone after her boss. Now that she'd seen her boss in full terrifying action, she couldn't support the man. His irrational fury had scared her witless.

As far as she was concerned, because Holden started them down this road, he could be the one to figure out why the Congressman lost his mind last night. Maybe he could help her stay out of jail, too.

Holden sure seemed strong enough. Even in sleep, he had an air of control blowing around him. She wasn't much for facial hair, but the stubble around his chin suited him. It added to his tough-guy effect.

"You're staring," he said in a low voice without opening his eyes.

She jumped off the mattress at the sound. "I didn't know you were awake."

"Am now." His eyes came open, showing the deep blue that transfixed her when they first met. "I'm a light sleeper."

"Good to know."

His eyebrow lifted. "Plan to use that information later, do you?"

"I'm ignoring that comment."

He lifted a hand and then let it drop. "Caleb says you're lucky you don't have a concussion."

"I'm not sure how lucky I feel, but it's good to know I didn't turn my brain into mush." She folded the sheet down to keep it away from her mouth. "Speaking of Caleb, your friends didn't look too pleased with your admission about watching Walters."

"They're not alone."

"What does that mean?" She shifted on the pillow to see him better and said a little thank-you when her head didn't rock back and forth.

"I knew when I started digging it was a

possibility Walters would come after me. Frankly, I welcomed it because the guy could use a takedown as far as I can tell." Holden sighed hard enough to shake the bed. "Just never expected he'd put the whole hacking incident on you."

"You didn't know I existed."

"True."

"Then how could you have anticipated me being in danger?"

"What?"

"This isn't your fault."

He looked at her this time. Really looked. "You're taking this well. I'd think most women would not be happy."

Holden and women. It wasn't the first time thoughts on that topic drifted into her head. She didn't know much about him. Hadn't seen a girlfriend. Tried to imagine what she—the imaginary other she—would think about him being in bed with Mia now.

"I'm too busy being disappointed about my boss and confused about what just happened to me," she said instead of asking the question she wanted to ask.

Holden's gaze caressed her face, so soft and caring she almost felt it against her skin. "I'm not sure how to apologize to you."

"Say you're sorry."

He chuckled. "Is it really that simple?"

"Seems to me people make things hard." Years of schooling and hours of helping people through therapy taught her that much.

"That's my experience, yes."

"It's clear you weren't trying to frame me." He started to say something, but she cut him off. "And I have a feeling you'll kick your butt harder for this than I ever could."

He smiled at that. "True."

"Did I ever thank you for saving my life?" She wanted to reach out and run her fingers along his jaw. Feel the rough edge of his shadow against her skin. She tucked her hand under the pillows to keep from trying.

"Did I tell you how sorry I am that piece of garbage in Rod's condo touched you?"

The memory sent a chill spinning through her. She clamped her eyes shut for a second to block the vision of dirty fingernails and a sharp blade. "Also not your fault."

"You noticing how bad things happen when you're with me?"

More guilt. He was loaded down with it. She didn't need her psychology degree to figure that one out. "Said the man with no house or worldly possessions."

"I should have stopped him."

"You did."

Holden was reliving the moments before he let the knife fly. She could almost see it play like a movie in his eyes. He wanted to pick at this, analyze it and figure out how he could have handled it differently.

She wanted to wipe it clear from her mind. Forever.

He swallowed hard enough for her to see his throat move. "You have to know I wouldn't—"

She scooted up even higher on the pillows and placed a finger over his lips. "I know."

With a gentle brush, Holden moved her palm from his mouth and slipped it against his. Lying there, so intimate in the cozy room, yet touching only through their joined hands. She was amazed at how something so pure and simple could wipe out a painful moment.

"He deserved to die for touching you." Holden kissed the back of her hand.

"Don't say that."

"I'm not proud of it, but I'm not going to apologize for how I feel either."

Because she could not work up guilt for her attacker's death, she switched to an area far more personal. "Would you do something for me?"

"If I can."

"Help me wipe away the feel of his touch."

He squeezed her hand in his. "In time that will fade."

Intellectually she knew that, but she wanted to fast-forward the process. To feel clean again. "I mean now."

"I don't—" Holden's voice cut off when she rested their joint hands on her chest, right above her breasts. "I'm not sure this is a good idea."

"Why?"

His breathing picked up, his chest rising and falling as he spoke. "You're upset. It might be too much too soon."

"I know what I want."

"Which is?"

"For you to touch me." She opened his fist, spreading his palm against hers and testing how much longer his fingers were than hers. "You're so big. Broad shoulders, huge hands."

"We barely know each other." His rough whisper filled the quiet room.

"You won't physically hurt me."

"Never."

"Look, I'm not the type to jump into bed with a stranger, but it feels right with you. And I need a different memory. A good one." She slid the tips of his fingers against her breast.

The warmth of his skin burned through her shirt and bra. He didn't try to cup her or increase his hold. He didn't rub or caress. He just let his body's heat seep into her as she learned his touch.

She didn't realize the mixed signals she sent until her shoulders relaxed against the bed. With one hand, she held him around the wrist and brought him close. The other pressed near his elbow, pushing him away.

"I'm sorry," she whispered.

"Don't be."

She eased her grip on his arm. The tiny half-moons her nails left on his flesh filled her with immediate regret. She rubbed her thumb over the evidence of her fear. An apology lingered on her tongue, but she bit it back when she saw his face.

His deep focus, his gaze centered on his hand and her breast underneath, broke through the nervous thoughts dancing around in her head. Instead of tolerating his touch, she craved it. This time her fingers moved over the back of his hand, shaping his palm around her.

"Are you sure?" he asked.

She nodded because that was all she could manage as she stared at the combination of his lightly tanned skin against the gray of her shirt. This was different. He was different.

When his hand gave her a gentle squeeze, her body kicked to life. The soft stroking wiped away the fear and pain of being mauled, replacing it with a building excitement, with a fresh burst of feeling that had everything to do with pleasure and nothing to do with pain.

"Tell me if I hurt you."

"You're good." She didn't even recognize the husky tone of her voice.

When she finally dragged her gaze away from the hand on her body and the soft caress of her skin, she saw those deep-blue eyes. He watched her, taking in her pleasure until the serious frown on his face smoothed.

"Kiss me," he said in a voice as rough as hers.

She lifted her head. With her mouth on his and the soft touch of his palm against her, she fell into the kiss. Warm lips. A soft moan. Fingers playing in her hair. The others skimming over the swell of her breast.

She let his embrace wash through her and

clear out the terrible memories of the day. There was only this. Right now.

When the kiss went deeper, it carried her right along with it. His lips crossed over hers as his breath rushed harder against her. Her hand slipped up to his neck to pull him closer just as his tongue slipped inside her mouth. In a matter of seconds they passed from easy comfort to white-hot heat.

Before she could blink, he turned his head and ended the kiss. Air rushed out of his lungs on a cough as he rested his forehead against hers.

"Wasn't expecting that." His thumb made one last pass over her nipple.

Her muscles ached with the need for more. "Me either."

"You need your rest." His lips traveled over her brows and down to her nose for a sweet kiss. "Now go to sleep."

"After that?"

He dragged his hand away from her, careful to smooth his fingers down the inside of her arm before breaking contact. Only his fingers in her hair continued the connection.

"Got a little carried away there," he said with a not-so-innocent smile.

"We could—"

"No." He planted a quick kiss on her mouth but pulled away before it could build to anything. "How's your head?"

"Cloudy?"

He pulled back and shot her a look of serious concern. "I'll call for Caleb."

She grabbed him before he could call in reinforcements. And he would. "From the kiss."

Understanding dawned on Holden's face. "You are tempting, but Caleb ordered you to sleep."

"What did he tell you to do?"

"He was upset with my meddling in the Walters issue at the time, so he didn't really say anything I can repeat without blushing."

She couldn't help but smile at the thought of that. "A big, tough guy like you? I can't imagine you blushing."

Holden wrapped his arm around her shoulders and pulled her in close to his side. "Besides, my job is to wake you up in two hours."

Rather than fight it, pretend she was fine, she snuggled against his warmth and inhaled the fresh scent of soap and shampoo on his skin. "Are you setting an alarm?"

"Don't need to. I've always been able to get up when I want to get up."

"That's quite a skill."

"One of many."

She peeked up at him. "That's good to know."

With a gentle touch, he pressed her head back against his shoulder. "Go to sleep before I forget to be a gentleman."

Chapter Nine

The alarm sounded at three in the morning. A buzzer rang through the house as the watch on Holden's wrist vibrated. Tuned to danger and accustomed to switching from sleep to get-up-and-fight mode, he sprang out of bed and reached for the gun on the nightstand.

His eyes adjusted to the dark within seconds. Figuring out the source of the danger took longer. He looked at the window, straining to see the fence at the end of the long drive. He could make out lights and trees and little else. Yet the alarm continued to rattle.

Mia shifted on the mattress, then sat straight up. With the sheet pressed to her chest, she glanced around the dark room. Her head turned back and forth fast enough to make even a person without a head injury get sick.

Pieces of hair hung in her eyes and the pink flush of sleep stained her skin when she honed in on him. "What's wrong?"

"Something."

Her eyes focused. "Could you be more specific?"

The door creaked the second before it flew open. Holden rounded on the entrance with his gun raised as he signaled for Mia to stay down.

Caleb came through the opening shouting a warning at the same time. "It's me."

Holden backed down the adrenaline pumping through his veins and forced his shoulders to unbunch. "That was close."

"No time to knock. We need to get downstairs." Caleb glanced at Mia. "Both of you."

Holden wanted to ask what had happened, but Caleb was gone.

"I don't understand," she said.

"Me either." Holden held out a hand to her. "But since Caleb isn't one to get upset over nothing, we need to move."

"Right." She didn't hesitate. She jumped out of bed wearing only panties and a T-shirt.

The flash of long legs grabbed his attention away from the alarm of the moment. If he'd known how little she had on when they kissed earlier, she'd be undressed by now.

When she pulled on the sweats, his focus

snapped back into place. "We go downstairs with you at my back. Do not move unless I tell you to."

"I'm not arguing with the chain of command."

"Good." He pivoted out the door and felt her fingers curl into the waistband of his jeans.

They slid along the banister with his hip balanced against the wood. Halfway down, he saw Caleb and Luke standing in the entry on either side of the front door.

Holden guided Mia to the bottom and beside Claire. "You the only two here?"

Luke nodded. "Adam and Zach went to check out some places around town for Rod."

So, they had three men to handle whatever was coming through the door. Holden felt comfortable with those odds. "What are we looking at here?"

Luke glanced at the small monitor on his wrist. "Four men in combat gear near the front gate."

"The plan?" Holden asked.

A smile broke across Luke's mouth. "Tick off the neighbors."

"They already hate the fence. Why not completely alienate them?" Claire mumbled.

"Imagine what they're going to say when the floodlights turn on." Luke held a small remote control in his hand.

Caleb glanced away from the outside for a second. "You think lights are going to scare these guys?"

"They're coming in soft. I'm guessing this is a test run on the security. So, we scare them off. But not before we try to catch one of them."

Holden understood the plan. They'd walked through it numerous times after Luke and Claire decided to move in and tried to establish a normal life. Divert and attack. Easy enough.

Holden started issuing orders before Luke could say anything. "Caleb and I will take opposite directions in front. I'll circle and provide a diversion while Caleb goes to work."

Luke had suffered a significant shoulder injury when he rescued Claire from her ex months before. He still didn't have full use of the arm, but he had an ego and didn't like getting stuck with desk duty. Holden knew they didn't have time to argue about who was best suited to skulk around in the darkness, so he made the decision for the group.

Mia stepped in front of Holden. "No."

Not the direction from which Holden expected a fight. From her pale skin and wide eyes, he knew she was terrified. She was about to be in the middle of another gun battle. Any smart person would worry, but he couldn't let that look stop him.

"It will be fine," he said.

She grabbed his arm, her nails biting into his skin. "You are volunteering to be a target."

Caleb raised his hand. "Then I'll do it."

"No," Holden snapped back. No way was he backing down from an assignment. Not for her or anyone else.

"Then it's settled." Luke nodded. "Holden will draw fire and I'll zap the gate. That should knock out anyone long enough for Caleb to grab him. Let's look to prevent gunfire and collateral damage."

Mia's hands were on her hips now. "And what if Holden gets shot in the process?"

Holden spared Luke from having to answer. "Not going to happen."

"You could call the police," she said.

"Not until we know why commandos are trying to storm an innocent-looking house in the middle of suburbia." Holden didn't wait for more questions. He picked up the black vest Claire held out for him and checked his weapons. No one was getting into this house on his watch.

"I'll feed intel from here and Claire will keep her hand on the phone in case we need to call 911." Luke glanced at the watch monitor again.

"That's not funny." Claire pulled Mia away from Holden and toward the dining room.

Luke ignored the comment and stayed focused on the screen. "We got one trying to get through the bars."

"Perfect." Holden motioned for Caleb to take the exit through the kitchen.

Holden was going through the front door. He wanted all eyes on him and all thoughts of Mia out of his head. She'd be safe in the house with Luke. Holden needed his mind on the guy trying to get to them.

Opening the door as little as possible, he slipped out and onto the front porch and ducked behind the pillar holding up one side of the small porch roof. He hadn't bothered with night goggles and regretted that choice. The cool weather and rolling clouds made the sky even darker than usual. In the distance he could make out shadows but not much else.

He made his way along the front of the

house, going left and keeping his body low and in-line with the bushes. His feet fell against the wet grass with a minimum of noise. The hope was to blend in until he got close enough for Luke to hit the button.

When Holden reached the far edge of the fence, his sight line to the front of the property opened. He didn't see Caleb but knew he was stationed opposite from him on the high wall. The plan was to curve around and hit the intruders from both sides. The green dots on Holden's watch indicated his team's movements and showed Luke safe in the house.

Everything went according to plan. Holden had reached the front of the property without being seen. From this angle, he watched two men working on the fence. One attempted to cut through the metal while the other kept guard.

This was easier than they imagined. One zap and the fence would come to life and knock them both out. Holden gave the signal to Luke.

Nothing happened.

Again, Holden hit the "go" button but the lights stayed off and the fence remained silent. He scanned the area looking for any signs of Caleb.

The yard couldn't be more than two acres. At this distance, communications should be up, but the opposite was true. Holden stood in the open, not fifty feet from the intruders, and could not reach his team.

He decided to try a new strategy: wound first, apologize later. The silencer would keep the commotion to a minimum, but he had to work fast. With two men out front, that left two unaccounted for. If they were on the property, they could be near the front door. Close to Mia and Claire.

That got him moving. He raised his weapon right as the intruders glanced up. After a long frozen look, the intruders backed away from the gate. Through his site, Holden watched them scatter, racing down the other side of the street and blending into the shadows around them.

Holden reached their previous point of entry in time to see dark figures slide into the black night. He ducked down, listening for footsteps or evidence of the other two. Nothing came back to him.

Continuing his circle, he found Caleb on his back on the ground about halfway back to the house. His gun was gone and blood trickled from his temple.

Holden dropped to the lawn. He watched the area around him as he felt for a pulse. Relief flooded through him when a strong beat pounded under his fingers. "Caleb."

The other man shifted and groaned. Finally his eyes popped open. "You okay?"

"I'm not the one who got hit." Holden helped his friend sit up. "What happened?"

Caleb rubbed his forehead. "Got jumped from behind."

"That means the intruders got inside the gate without Luke knowing." Holden didn't understand how something like that was possible. Only the team had the code. Between the alarms and protections, a breach should have been impossible.

"If someone breached, then why were the other two hanging out on the opposite side of the front gate."

They got played. That fact zoomed right into Holden's brain. "Those two were the diversion."

The daze started to clear from Caleb's eyes. "Where are the ones who hit me?"

The truth smacked Holden like a sucker punch to the stomach. "The house!"

They took off at a run, their footsteps fast yet quiet. Without saying a word, they knew they had to work in unison and reach the front door as fast as possible.

Somehow Holden slowed his heart. Racing in and getting everyone killed wasn't a decent plan. He put all thoughts of Mia out of his head and concentrated on listening for any sound bouncing back to him.

They rounded the porch. The door stood wide open and the remote control lay on the porch. With a simple hand signal, Holden sent Caleb to the left as he walked through the main entrance.

Holden took the right. No signs of struggle. No blood.

A slight creak of the floorboards sounded above them. Both Caleb and Holden reacted to the noise. Holden waited as Caleb checked the kitchen and small den at the back of the house. He came back into the entry and shook his head.

That meant the intruders went in one of two directions, up to the bedrooms or down to the underground control room. Since the bottom floor of the house wasn't on any building plan anywhere and the entrance was nearly impossible to find without knowing about it Holden bet the armed men went up instead.

He nodded to Caleb, then hit the first stair.

With slow, steady steps, Holden went up, pausing on every riser to listen for signs of life. As he watched, legs clad in dark pants moved into his line of vision.

On the landing and with the advantage from above, the intruder turned and fired. The wall behind Holden's head blew apart and his foot slipped off the step.

Off balance, he pumped two bullets. The first slammed into the man's chest, pushing him back with a grunt. The second hit his leg.

Holden reached the man right as he fell to his back. As Holden shifted to kick the weapon away, a second man rushed out of the bedroom Holden had shared with Mia. He saw a flash of black clothing right before Caleb rushed up the stairs, firing as he ran. Almost instantly a red blotch spread across the intruder's forehead. Momentum kept him moving as he went flying over the banister and crashed against the first-floor tile with a sharp smack.

When Holden turned back, he saw the man he shot wrestling to sit up and reaching for his gun. Holden didn't hesitate. This time he skipped the chest and obvious protective vest the man wore and followed Caleb's lead and went for the head.

People talk about disasters moving in slow motion. To Holden, it zipped by even faster than usual. With not even a second to breathe or think, he reacted. Movements flowed into each other. Shoot, duck, aim.

Now as he focused on the rushing beat of his heart, he glanced around at the bloody aftermath. In the span of five minutes, the shoot-out had ended. Two intruders lay dead on the floor and three people were still missing.

Holden looked to the bottom of the staircase and edited that number to two. Luke stood there, gun raised and ready to provide backup.

"Everyone okay?" Luke's voice took Caleb by surprise and had him spinning.

"Whoa." Holden put his hand on Caleb's arm and lowered his gun.

"What the hell happened?" Caleb's words raced out.

"Something jammed the signal," Holden said. "It was as if they got into our communication system."

Luke lowered his weapon. "I saw the two come up the lawn as you went down. My priority was getting Mia and Claire out of the firing line."

Holden didn't care about the logistics. "Where is Mia?"

"Here." She popped out from around the banister. She twisted the edge of her T-shirt in her fingers but otherwise appeared calm.

He tried to beat back the energy still pumping through him. The blonde in front of him helped. Seeing her alive and safe put a lid on his frustration. Breathing returned to normal. Once he could convince his fingers to ease up on his gun, he'd be fine.

"How'd they breech the perimeter?" Caleb asked.

Luke's calm demeanor slipped for a second before he regained control. "No idea. According to my readings, everything held, but that's clearly not the case."

Claire held out her arms and gestured around her. "Apparently not."

Luke grimaced. "Sorry about this."

Claire wasn't ready to be dismissed. "Look at my house."

"We'll figure it out. I'll put Adam on it and we'll have an answer in no time." Luke tucked his gun in his waistband with enough force to rip the fabric. "Nothing like this is ever going to happen again."

Claire's mouth flattened into a straight line. "If you say so."

Luke stared at his wife. "I promise."

Holden understood the fury battering Luke. He had vowed to keep his wife safe. They all had. Two men got within feet of her and Mia. Reality beat the crap out of the idea they were prepared and in control of the situation.

Inside they were all burning with frustration. Two private residences violated in two days. This was about more than shutting down Recovery Project. Someone was coming after each of them. This was personal.

Mia stood next to the dead man's hand. "How do we get around calling the police now? The bodies are starting to pile up."

Luke kicked the man's foot. "Rod usually takes care of this part."

Claire stared up at her broken banister. "Then we better find him so I can have my house back."

Holden knew she was struggling to find normal. He also knew that was gone forever.

Chapter Ten

Bram Walters sat at the massive cherry desk in his office the next morning. Outside his door, staffers hunkered down in their cubicles, answering calls and mail. The flag hung from a pole behind his head and the walls were lined with photos of Bram with visiting dignitaries and heroes from his district in Virginia.

He'd dreamed of this job, this chair, and now he'd achieved it. He held the power. After paying his dues and consistently voting with his party's leadership, he'd moved to the top. He had his pick of choice committee assignments.

And a small group of people could ruin all that. Destroy him.

He rubbed his sore shoulder. Mia dislocated it when she hit him with the car. Popping it back into place had hurt more than the broken ribs. If she had just answered him when he asked about her partners none of this would have happened. He could have turned her, used her as his inside spy. But not now.

If only he had refused to hire her in the first place.

The entire tense situation he now found himself in started with a favor. Then it spun into a tragedy when Trevor's ex-wife decided to use the divorce and their son as weapons of personal destruction. Now Bram was stuck dealing with blackmail dressed up as obligation.

His main assignment was clear: crush the Recovery Project group so they couldn't ask questions. Discredit Rod Lehman and his work. The Project's previous handling of the Claire Samson, now Hathaway, incident made that task easier. No one on the intelligence subcommittee liked the idea of a rogue law-enforcement team receiving federal funding and not being subjected to any rules.

But he had a deeper problem. Doing a favor for Steve Samson was one thing. Getting roped into tracking down the top-secret whereabouts of individuals covered by witness relocation was a different type of disaster, one Bram could only indirectly trace back to Steve.

But all led back to the Recovery Project.

If he got caught poking around in WitSec

files it wouldn't matter that he was forced to do it or that Trevor's inappropriate request for help in his custody fight led to the mess. Bram knew he would be the one to hang. He'd lose everything. That's why it was so important to keep his blackmailer and make sure Mia and the Recovery Project team stayed out of his life.

"Well?" Bram asked his brother.

Trevor continued to hum as he leaned back in the plush light blue armchair and read the report from the file in front of him. For a man whose personal life had fallen apart a year before, he was remarkably unruffled.

But Bram wasn't accustomed to waiting for answers. When he asked questions, people responded. He had the power to fire eager young Capitol Hill staffers and subpoena even the most powerful to appear in front of his intelligence subcommittee.

Trevor closed the folder. "Mia is alive."

The last flicker of hope died in Bram. "You're sure?"

"All the bodies are accounted for and all were my men. The owner of the house got away with Mia."

"Who is the owner?"

Trevor tapped his fingers against the manila

file. "Now that's the interesting part. It's Holden Price."

"So, it all comes back to the Recovery Project." Bram slammed a fist against his desk. "I knew it. Any progress on that end? I need to find them all and contain them."

"The codes to the Hathaway house worked on the trial run. My men were able to get in and close, but I lost two. Important thing is Hathaway and his team now know they're being watched."

The dead bodies all seemed to belong to Trevor. Bram worried the results were a testament to the Recovery agents' abilities. "How are you going to explain the deaths?"

"Training accident."

"You think Hathaway is going to go along with that story after you breached his security?"

Trevor wore an expression that hovered between pity and contempt. "You still don't understand these men."

"My job is to break them, not admire them."

"The reason you hate them is the same reason they're so successful," Trevor said with more than a touch of admiration in his voice. "They work outside of the rules. That's why you're pushing for the group's dissolution, correct? Steve needs them out of the way to have a chance at trial and our contact just needs them gone."

Bram refused to play this game where Trevor pretended he had nothing to do with the trouble they now wallowed in. Trevor was under the same pressure. Acting otherwise ticked Bram off.

"You know why I'm holding the hearings. I don't have a choice," he said.

"You're the one who did the favor for Steve Samson and started us down this road."

Bram didn't need to be reminded what his friendship with the Samson brothers had cost him. "I am aware of my role. Do you remember yours?"

"We did get lucky on one point. Luke Hathaway is a smart man. He doesn't want police swarming all over him and that cozy setup of his. He disposed of the bodies from his lawn." Trevor smiled. "If he could trace them back to me, he'd probably dump them at my doorstep."

Bram felt his temper blow. "Could you manage to be less enamored with the Recovery agents since they are making my life hell at the moment?"

"Holden Price blew up his house, shot my men and escaped with the girl. It's hard not to have some admiration."

Bram knew he wouldn't get anywhere with that conversation. "Any casualties for the Recovery team from the raid?"

"No."

He slammed his hand against his desk. "How is that possible?"

"As I said, don't underestimate them."

Holden and Luke and the others might outshoot and outrun their opponents, but outside of their comfort zone it might be a different story. "Then it's time to apply more pressure."

Trevor nodded. "Agreed. We need to keep the team busy, drive them further apart."

"I'm issuing subpoenas for all of them to appear before my committee."

"Smart. You bring the team in and I'll smoke out Ms. Landers."

Finally Trevor regained his priorities. Bram was grateful for the change. "How?"

"Your loyal office worker is missing. Seems to me you might want to make a public plea for her safe return."

He could play the role of worried employer

and send a message at the same time. "I like it."

"And her ex-boyfriend can help."

"Who is that?" Bram wasn't convinced they needed another player in this game.

"A former policeman. He's unemployed, but I'm thinking I can find him some work."

Bram thought about Mia but then pushed all concern aside. "Do I want to know?"

"As usual, no."

Bram pressed the intercom button. His door opened a second later. His upstanding and loyal chief of staff walked in. With his navy suit and perfect grooming, in a very short time David had worked his way up from intern to running an office.

"Can I get you something, sir?" David asked.

"I'm feeling much better. Next time I'll watch where I run and won't fall." Bram flashed his brother a warning glance. "Has Ms. Landers showed up for work yet?"

"No. I haven't been able to reach her at home or on her cell. She doesn't have any family and the emergency contacts she listed haven't heard from her in quite some time."

"I'm worried about her." Bram was impressed—he sounded so genuine in his concern.

"Agreed. She's very responsible. Missing work without any explanation is well out of the norm."

"Right. Keep me posted." Bram nodded to let David know he should leave.

Trevor waited until the door closed to laugh. "You said you were running?"

"Injuries from a car accident would have been too hard to explain. Too many questions and potential problems about the lack of a police report."

"True."

"In a few hours I'll make a public plea for Mia to return my call."

"That should put some pressure on."

HOLDEN LOWERED the volume on the television and sat down hard on the couch next to Mia.

Mia shook her head. "That's not possible."

Adam leaned forward on the edge of his chair and tapped his fingers together. "Walters is clearly alive. He's right there on television and talking about how worried he is about you."

She was not insane. She knew what happened

out in those woods and could call up the visual details without even trying. "I hit him with my car."

Claire snorted as she dropped onto the armrest of the couch next to her husband. "Of course you did. Does anyone believe that guy jogs? He's about thirty pounds overweight and soft as a donut."

"He's pretending I'm missing." Mia was stunned at the idea. Why, she didn't know. The Congressman had done so many unbelievable things lately.

"He's sending you a secret message. Telling you he's not done," Caleb said from his position leaning against the fireplace mantel.

Holden shook his head. "The message is for us, not her."

Mia still didn't understand how all the pieces fit together. Sure, her boss wanted to ruin the men in this room. She got that. And, yes, Holden's computer tricks made her look guilty. But why all the trouble? The Congressman had power and money. He didn't need to pick fights.

She stared at Holden. "How does he even know I'm with you? You hacked the computer, but with all your covert mumbo jumbo how does the trail lead back to you?"

Holden shrugged. "He has resources. His brother's company can track anything down. For whatever reason, Trevor is using his men as a private army and backing Bram's actions."

"Risky maneuver since most people view Trevor as a legitimate operator. He has the government contracts to prove it," Caleb said.

"We sure the Congressman didn't deliver those contracts?" Adam asked. "Maybe this is a little brotherly payback."

"Probably, but the point is Trevor has resources." Holden exhaled. "By now they know the cabin was mine and added together his congressional investigation and my role in Recovery and decided Mia was working undercover for me."

"But why come after us?" Caleb left the fireplace and took a seat next to Luke. "We're not a threat to Trevor's company."

"We're a threat to someone," Luke said.

Adam kept tapping those fingers. "Rod sure was."

"Is." Holden's voice shook with fury. With a red face and locked jaw, he looked ready to kill.

Mia took it all in and still didn't get it.

Didn't like the look on Holden's face either. If he spoke to her in that tone, she'd be paralyzed. She'd lived with a man who thought that was an appropriate way to speak with a loved one. He never used his fists, but his sharp words inflicted incredible damage.

Adam didn't seem to notice the tension in the room. "You should have seen Rod's place in western Maryland. Someone ripped it apart. Smashed floorboards, holes in the ceiling."

"It's true." Those were the only words Zach had uttered since he entered the house an hour ago.

He and Adam returned from Rod's farm with drawn faces. The demolition they described left Mia believing Rod met with a terrible end.

"Anything Rod hid is gone now."

All of the men frowned at Adam's comment.

After a beat of silence, Luke spoke up again. "At least we know how the intruders got in here."

Mia wasn't sure how they jumped to that conclusion. "We do?"

"Rod has our personal information," Adam explained. "He kept it in lockdown, but he definitely had it out on his farm."

The importance of the violation settled deep in her stomach. It meant the end of safety and privacy. Tall fences and underground rooms weren't going to fix this.

"Now the Congressman has it," she said.

"We'll change the codes and switch frequencies." Luke patted his wife's knee, then stood up. "In the meantime, everyone needs to check their own place and clear out any identifying information. We'll meet back here and go through the documents Rod saved to our internal system. There might be a clue of some sort in there as to what he was doing or where he might be."

Claire smiled at Mia. "You can stay here."

"She comes with me." Holden made the comment before Claire finished hers.

Luke frowned at the suggestion. "People will be looking for her."

Holden jumped on that, too. "I want her where I can see her."

Found it. She'd been wondering about the downside of having all these strong and protective men milling around. Now she knew. A man like Holden demanded to be in charge. He pushed and shoved and generally got his way.

The controlling behavior brought unpleasant

memories rolling back over her in waves. She'd been down this road and had lost all sense of her own mind. She began doubting her instincts and conceding decisions to a boyfriend who insisted he be in charge.

She lost her friends and her sense of self. Even now she struggled with having her voice heard. Although she trusted Holden with her safety—all of them, really—he needed to know she had a mind and planned on using it.

"Anyone care about what Mia wants?" Mia asked, letting the sarcasm drip off her voice.

Claire raised her hand. "I do."

"I decide." When Holden opened his mouth to argue with her, Mia raced through the rest of her thought. "It is my life and my body. The choice is mine."

The anger simmering under the surface at the talk of Rod being dead exploded. Holden sputtered as if searching for words while his friends stared in stunned confusion.

She finally put him out of his misery. "And I've made a decision."

"Which is?" Luke asked.

"I've decided I'll stick with Holden."

Chapter Eleven

The stale scent hit Holden as soon as he opened the door. He hadn't been in his place in the city for weeks. The lack of fresh air left the place looking and smelling even less inviting than usual.

He walked over to the sliding glass door in the small family room and pushed the curtains open. The move let the light in and allowed him to make sure no one stood out there.

"Not as nice as Luke's place, but it serves its purpose," Holden said.

Mia ran her hand across the top of the cushions of his apartment-size sectional sofa. Other than the television, there was nothing else in the room. The furniture came with the one-bedroom place and Holden never bothered to change it.

"Quite the bachelor pad." Her tone let him know what she thought of his taste.

"If you say so."

She sat on the armrest and watched him move around the space. "Is anyone looking for you?"

The hesitation in her voice caught his attention. She wasn't one to weigh words. Or she hadn't been so far.

"Excuse me?"

"Your house blew up. I'd think family— someone—would want to make sure you're okay."

They'd finally reached the snooping, personal part of the program. He wondered when her curiosity would kick in. He didn't have to fight the same internal battle. Luke had told Holden everything he needed to know about Mia. Having the inside information felt a bit like cheating, but Holden justified his actions by convincing himself the background search protected his team.

The paperwork on her confirmed her as an innocent pawn. She was smart with a doctorate degree in psychology, a fact that scared the hell out of him. Last thing he needed was a woman dissecting his feelings in the bedroom.

And they were going to end up in bed. It was just a matter of finding the right time and a half hour of privacy. Hard to concentrate on enjoying the moment when men hunted them down and people roamed everywhere in Luke's house and could open a bedroom door by accident.

She was the only and late-in-life child of parents who died one after the other a few years ago. An adult orphan who lived first with a cop and now lived alone. That last part was the only fact that mattered to Holden. No ties to another man.

Because she wore a serious frown, he decided to tweak her. "Are you asking me if I have a girlfriend?"

"Where did you hear that question?" She twisted her fingers together on her lap. Much harder and she might snap one off.

"I was interpreting."

"More like wishful thinking." She snorted not once but twice.

When she let loose with that annoying sound he seriously considered making her ask him directly for the information. "If you say so."

"Are you familiar with the psychological term narcissism?"

Oh, no. Of all the things he wanted from her, psychobabble was not one of them. He'd been diagnosed after the incident in

Afghanistan. Five-hundred-pound bombs and six hours of fighting trapped him near Khost in the Uruzgan province. Seven days in a collapsed mountain cave with two dead soldiers from Charlie Company lying at his feet.

He'd been down that road with mental-health professionals who vowed to "cure" him. He had no intention of driving there again. "No girlfriend."

Her mouth opened and then clamped shut. It wasn't until he sent her a look that dared her to comment that she tried. "I didn't ask."

"I wanted you to know."

"Oh."

"I have a father in Arizona but no girlfriend."

She shrugged. "Why would that matter to me?"

For a woman with formal training, she sure could be clueless about men and their desires. Either that or this amounted to a big game of hard to get.

He lowered his eyebrows and stared her down. "Come on. Really? I find it hard to believe you don't know the answer to that one."

She nearly jumped off the couch. One second she sat there fidgeting yet trying to act cool. The next she paced in front of his balcony door. "You could open this and let some fresh air in."

"No."

"No?"

"This is a city."

"Not to bring up a touchy subject, but I got chased and nearly killed in the country where you live."

"Can't argue with that." He tried the most logical arguments at his disposal. "But it's also cold out and there are trained killers lurking around."

"I guess that's true." She crossed her arms over her stomach. The body language flashed a female "keep out" sign. But those smoky eyes suggested something else.

"Happy to impress you."

She smirked. "I never said I was impressed."

Just when he decided to put an end to the sexual torture and take her to bed, a knock at the door crushed the moment. The amusement growing inside him faded away, replaced by a readiness that stayed with him as an ingrained instinct even after military retirement.

He had the gun out and aimed at the front of his condo before the second tap sounded. With a nod of his head he motioned for her to hide in the bedroom. He mouthed the word *closet* and started for the entry.

Keeping his body out of a firing line through the dead center of the door, he leaned over and looked out the peephole. Blue uniform. Gun holstered at the side. A policeman. That made as little sense as everything else that had happened over the past few days.

"Mr. Price? This is Detective Ned Zimmer of the Metropolitan Police Department."

The visit just got more interesting. Holden recognized the name. Hard not to since he just saw it in the report Luke handed him about Mia.

Holden shoved his gun in his back waistband. He wanted the weapon close until he knew what was happening. There was no need to antagonize by aiming at the officer, even though a screaming rush of jealousy begged him to do it.

Holden opened the door just far enough to look out. "Yes?"

"May I come in?"

"What is this about?"

Zimmer glanced down the hallway and back again. "Your house in Virginia, sir."

The conversation took a turn into pure deception. Zimmer was with the D.C. Police. His territory did not include the Virginia suburbs. Despite that, Holden backed up so the other man could come inside.

Immediately Zimmer scanned the room, his gaze sliding over every corner, which did not take very long. When the looking stopped the walking began. He slipped deeper into the family room and peeked into the bedroom.

"What's this about?" Holden asked.

"You own a piece of property in Fredericksburg, correct?"

All of a sudden everyone knew about his property ownership. A man couldn't buy a beat-up cabin in private. "Why would you think that?"

Zimmer's palm moved to the top of his gun. "Is that a yes, sir?"

"I live here."

"After some digging it's become clear you have a few acres south of the city, as well."

"And?"

Zimmer's gaze kept going to the bedroom. "The Fredericksburg police force asked me to contact you for a wellness check."

That was a nice touch. Almost believable. "That's interesting."

"I regret to inform you there's been an accident at your house."

Holden was impressed with the smooth and even tone. "You're in my house."

"The other one." Zimmer rocked back on his heels and strained to see past the half-closed bedroom door. The move was subtle but noticeable. "A fire. The structure was destroyed."

"Anyone hurt?"

"Not to my knowledge."

Holden could play this game all day. "Anything else?"

Zimmer focused on Holden then. "There's a missing woman."

"Who?"

"Mia Landers."

Walters or someone connected to him got to Zimmer. That was the only explanation Holden could see. Adam kept checking for formal investigations into Mia's disappearance and nothing turned up. So far, only Walters and Zimmer were talking about her being missing.

"There's some suggestion she was on your property before the explosion," Zimmer said.

Only someone who was there or involved in the planning of the attack would know about Mia being in Virginia. Walters could be fishing to see if she was alive, but Holden thought it was more likely Walters and Zimmer wanted to know where she hid.

"Is there also a suggestion I was at this house when the fire happened?" Holden asked. "As you can see, I'm not singed anywhere."

"Do you think this is a joke, sir?"

Pure cop tone. A bit frustrated and condescending yet outwardly respectful. Holden recognized the M.O. because he'd seen and heard it growing up with his cop father. "Not at all."

"Do you know Mia Landers?"

"No."

Zimmer hesitated. "Make I take a look around?"

"No."

Zimmer smacked his lips together. "Do you have something to hide?"

"I don't." Holden stepped into Zimmer's line of sight when the man shifted too close to the bedroom door. "And I wouldn't do that."

"Why?"

"I haven't given you permission to snoop around my place."

"You want me to get a warrant?"

They both knew that was am empty threat.

"If you think you have probable cause for something, be my guest."

Zimmer took one final look around and then headed to the door. Reaching into his pocket, he pulled out a card. "If you see Ms. Landers, call me at this number."

Holden didn't even look at it. He was too busy shutting the door behind Zimmer. "Absolutely."

MIA'S HANDS SHOOK so hard it took her three tries to open the folding door of the closet.

The screen screeched along the track as Holden opened it for her. He hovered in the doorway. "You dated that guy?"

"How did you know that?"

"Maybe you've missed the general gist of what I do for a living."

"You investigated me." She shoved past him and went to the bed. She had to sit down before her knees gave out.

"I needed to make sure you weren't a nut. In my defense, you drove through my front door."

"You're just not going to let that go."

"I don't see that happening, no." Holden shifted his weight as he spoke.

Mia realized he was nervous. He actually

thought she was furious about the privacy violation. In reality she trembled because the sound of Ned's voice had that hold over her. Even now, after months of being apart and standing in Holden's protective shield, Ned had the power to stop her internal organs from functioning. His angry phone calls of a week ago still rang in her ears.

"He strikes me as a loser." Holden followed her to the mattress and sat down next to her.

"He is, which is why he's my ex." She refused to use her ex's name. He didn't deserve any power over her and recognizing him in any way would do that. "That brings me to the other issue."

"Which is?"

She leaned her shoulder against Holden's, gaining confidence from his muscled arm. "He's no longer with the police department."

Holden pulled back so fast, he had to put an arm out and catch her. "Are you sure?"

"I was at the hearing."

"Care to explain that?"

"His fitness hearing."

Holden slid a hand over her thigh in a move that calmed the nerves jumping around inside of her. "What did he do?"

"Roughed up a witness." But that was just

one of Ned's many missteps. He was the kind of man who thrived on power and abused it when he had it.

"You were there because…?"

"I testified about how he bragged about the incident."

Holden whistled. "That would sure give the man a reason not to like you. It also means my radar isn't off. I didn't like him from the second he walked in here."

"And this was one of his good days."

Holden's hand tightened on her leg for a fraction of a second before it eased. "Did he ever hurt you?"

"Not physically."

"I'm not sure I like that answer."

They were even because she hated everything about Ned. "He called me last week to let me know I ruined his life."

"Interesting."

She couldn't tell if that was a judgment or a statement. The idea of Holden siding with Ned stabbed through her, puncturing her lungs and stealing her breath. "So, knowing all of that, why was he here and pretending to be on the job?"

"My guess? Walters knows about your history with Zimmer and is using it to scare you and warn me."

She regretted ever taking the congressional job. It was a huge step backward and a significant financial hit—on top of all this. "Is there anything Walters doesn't know?"

"I wouldn't count on that." Holden slipped his phone out of his back pocket. "How dangerous is Zimmer?"

"I'm not sure. I used to think he was just a bully, but he sounded desperate last I heard from him. From my experience, people get caught and act out."

"So, let me try this again. Did he threaten you?"

Not in the way Holden was suggesting. Ned was too smart for that. "He blames me."

"You're still not answering me."

"He's not worth a second of our time."

"I'll take that as a yes. Disgusting piece of garbage." Holden added a string of profane words to his description of her ex. "He's not going to try anything with me around."

A light flutter started in the bottom of her stomach at the idea Holden might stay around. She pushed out the possibility she amounted to nothing more than a duty or another person for him to rescue.

Holden hit a button and lifted the phone to his ear. "I'll call Adam and start him digging on Zimmer."

Cold snapped through her. "Fine."

"We have to get out of here without your boyfriend following us."

"Don't call him that."

Holden blew out a long, rough breath. "Sorry. I want to beat the crap out of the guy and am trying to send that energy somewhere else."

"While you're apologizing for stuff, think about asking for forgiveness for how easily you lie." She knew that was part of the job and meant to keep her safe, but the way the words so easily fell off his tongue without thought or hesitation scared her.

Holden's arm slowly fell to his side. "The thing I told Zimmer about knowing you?"

"That's the one. Yes."

"That was for your protection."

"Men always say that."

Chapter Twelve

Holden knew Zimmer lurked nearby. He could feel it, sense it. He wished he could gauge Mia's mood as easily. Ever since hearing Zimmer's voice, she'd been distant and jumpy.

That ticked Holden off. It felt like a lack of trust in his abilities. She had to know he'd keep her safe from the guy. Surely he'd earned at least that much credit by now.

"Are you ready to go?" she asked as she walked out of the bedroom and right by him.

He stopped her with a hand on her arm. "What's wrong with you?"

"My ex and my boss are hunting me down. I've seen I don't even know how many dead bodies. Surely you can understand where that would be disconcerting." She didn't yank her arm away, but after a small shift he was holding nothing but air.

"You get used to it."

"This isn't funny, Holden."

"Do I look like I'm laughing?" When she tried to answer his question, he stopped her. "We're not going to argue about this here."

"Why not?"

No reason to lie about this. Standing there in what felt like the wide open made the back of his neck itch. At his cabin he had weapons and contingency plans. Here he had an entrance and a potential unwelcome flight off the balcony.

"Being here makes me edgy. Okay? I'll feel better when we're back at Luke's house where there are other people and not such an open shot inside." He pointed at the sliding door and the gray sky beyond.

"That's what this is about? You think we're in danger."

"I know we are."

Her battle stance relaxed. Holden knew they'd walked through some sort of emotional minefield right there. He didn't know what had happened to make her mad and then to calm her back down again. Through clenched fists and a strained tone, she let him know she fought with rough doubts.

"So, what do we do?" she asked.

"You're going to stay in here and I'm going to check the hallway and stairs."

"For Ned."

"Exactly."

A little intel first. He called down to the lobby and asked the doorman if a police officer was hanging around. The answer didn't surprise him.

He flipped the phone closed and glanced at Mia. Nothing he had to say was going to wipe the pained expression off her face, but he needed her to know what was happening. "Zimmer never came back downstairs. Guess that means he's waiting for me up here somewhere."

"What if you find him?"

"Part of me hopes I do." Holden had a list of things he wanted to do to Zimmer. A man who beat up on women, physically or verbally, deserved a smackdown. Maybe if Ned's face hit the pavement a few times, he'd think twice about hurting a female again.

She exhaled as she slid in front of him. With her hands on his biceps, she tipped her head up and kissed his chin.

Not good enough. Holden didn't want chaste from her. Before she could back away, he covered her mouth with his. First deep and then lingering, he let his lips tell her his plans for later.

"Be careful," she whispered against his mouth as he broke away.

"Always."

He had to go. Having a bed so close and danger all around made for a mixed message his lower half couldn't interpret.

After a quick look out the peephole, Holden opened the door. He expected to find Zimmer hiding in a stairwell, but the guy turned out to be smarter than he looked.

The door slammed back, bouncing against Holden's head. The hit had him reeling. He stumbled back. Off balance, he tried to put his body between Zimmer and Mia.

"Hello, Mia." Zimmer's smile could only be described as feral, like a starved wild animal seeing food for the first time in weeks.

The tiny explosions stopped shooting off in Holden's brain, but he didn't let on. Better for Zimmer to think he had a wounded man in front of him.

Zimmer pointed his gun at Mia's head. "You're not a good liar, Mr. Price."

"You're not a very good cop, so we're even."

"Mia, come here." Zimmer's clenched teeth made his voice even lower and raspier than before. "You're going to pat down Mr. Price for me."

"No."

"I'm not playing games. Do it now."

"Who are you working for?" Holden asked as he shuffled his feet and backed up closer to Mia. If he had to throw his body in front of hers, take every bullet and kick, he'd do it.

Zimmer ignored Holden. He kept his harsh frown centered on Mia. "You've upset some powerful people and need to come in and answer questions."

"She's not going anywhere with you."

Zimmer pointed to his weapon. "I'm the one with the gun, Price. You are not in charge here."

"For now."

"You think you can take it from me?"

That's it. Take the bait. Holden knew this guy's ego wouldn't allow him to lose in front of Mia. "Something like that."

"You don't have the balls to rush me."

"I wouldn't count on that."

"Mia, now." Zimmer shifted his aim to Holden's chest. "Unless you want your new boyfriend to die in front of you."

"You're killing innocent men now?" She took a step forward.

Holden reached out his hand and held her back. The chance of wrestling the gun away from Zimmer decreased to single digits if he had Mia in his arms. Holden would never risk her life. He'd have to abandon his plan to tackle this jerk, and that's all he wanted to do at the moment. That and put a bullet through the guy's small brain.

"That's close enough to the crazy cop." Holden sent a warning with his tone and the stiffness of his arm.

"We don't have a choice." Her fingers rested against his back and then moved lower. "I can't let him hurt you and he's the only one with a gun."

Zimmer barked out a harsh laugh. "Listen to the woman."

"I have a name." Her fingers brushed against the top of Holden's waistband.

Only one reason she'd be touching him there right now. His weapon.

She drummed out a countdown on the metal handle, sending a vibration through him. A mix of panic and admiration thrummed in his blood. She might be afraid, but she was going down swinging.

As the gun slipped from its position, Holden dived. Arms out, he plowed into the other man's knees, knocking them backward at an angle guaranteed to inflict the most pain.

Zimmer's arms flew up as he lost control of the situation. The crunch of bone mixed with his shout of fury as he dropped the gun.

Holden kept fighting. He kicked Zimmer's weapon, sending it spinning across the wood floor in Mia's direction. With a knee on Zimmer's stomach, Holden held him down. Not that the man was fighting back. Zimmer wailed and swore. He panted and grabbed for his leg as he tried to curl in a ball around Holden's body.

Not such a tough guy now. Holden glanced up to share the thought with Mia and saw for the first time she was ready. She stood, legs apart, with the gun aimed right at Zimmer's forehead. Holden knew she couldn't shoot, but she sure looked as if she would if she had to.

Satisfaction filled his chest. "Nice."

"You broke my damn leg." Zimmer writhed around, slipping against the floor as he tried to get traction to sit up.

"I wish, but I doubt it." With a hard shove, Holden turned Zimmer over and slammed his chest against the floor.

Hearing the man groan in pain actually

felt good. Holden didn't analyze the murderous rage pounding in his head. It was simple enough to figure out. He'd been trained to serve and protect, but a man who played on a woman's fears didn't deserve his respect.

Snatching his handcuffs, Holden had the other man bound in a matter of seconds and turned him around. With his fingers wrapped in Zimmer's lapels, Holden slid him to a sitting position and leaned him against the wall.

Zimmer sucked in air as he rocked his shoulders back and forth against the wall. "You're going to pay for this."

"I doubt that." Holden stepped over the odd angle of Zimmer's leg and put his palm over Mia's hands. Slowly he lowered her arms until the gun pointed toward the floor.

"Assaulting a police officer is—"

"Shut up!" Mia flew at Zimmer. She would have gotten to him, too, if Holden hadn't placed his hands on her shoulders and pulled her back.

Holden loved this fiery protective side of her. "Easy now."

Her focus stayed on her ex. "You're not a cop. Not anymore."

When Zimmer ground out a nasty name for Mia, Holden decided it was time the guy learned a lesson. Holden lowered his foot and pressed it against Zimmer's injury. The resulting squealing shout would make someone come running. Holden was sure of that.

With time ticking away, Holden skipped to the next part of his plan. He grabbed for his phone.

"What are you doing?" Mia asked.

"Insurance." He snapped a photo. "If Zimmer here decides to complain or starts talking about assault charges, he can explain why he showed up here wearing a police uniform."

For the first time since Zimmer arrived, Mia smiled. "His former bosses would love that. Imagine how fast everyone would cut him loose."

"And I'm pretty sure pretending to be a police officer and assaulting someone with a gun is a crime. Can't imagine what would happen to Zimmer here in jail, what with some of the lies he's told to put his fellow criminals in there."

Zimmer spit. "You son of a—"

Holden crouched down until he was face-to-face with Zimmer. "We're going to come to an understanding."

"Take the handcuffs off."

Holden pressed his hand against Zimmer's crooked leg and waited while the man doubled over with a vicious growl.

"You're going to go back to your boss and tell him to leave Mia alone." Holden knew that wouldn't stop Walters, but it should warn him that Holden's role in this mess was no longer a secret.

Mia now had someone on her team, someone who wasn't afraid of a congressional seal. Walters had a lot to lose. He needed to understand that he was the only one who did.

Zimmer bared his teeth. "You can—"

"Then you're going to go away because if I see or hear about you coming near Mia, I'll kill you." Holden glanced at Mia and noticed she didn't seem upset by the threat.

Zimmer threw back his head, his neck muscles straining as he spoke. "She's not worth the load of crap that's going to come down on you over this."

Mia sighed. "You never did appreciate me."

"I got you. Had you," Zimmer said. "You weren't worth—"

Holden increased the pressure on Zimmer's leg. That was more than enough of that as far as Holden was concerned. "You would be wise to stop talking or I'll go ahead and kill you now."

Zimmer ground his teeth together. "You won't."

"Don't tempt me." Holden refused to let Zimmer take shots, not when all words like that did was make Holden want to beat the guy to death. He stood up and hooked his fingers under Mia's elbow. "Time to go."

"What about him?" Her tone stayed flat, as if she was asking about a dinner reservation instead of Zimmer's future.

"He has an hour to get out of here on his own. After that, I'll take care of it."

She nodded. "I almost hope he fails."

Chapter Thirteen

Mia walked into the Hathaways' house and felt all the stress leave her body. Melted right on the floor in front of her.

Seeing Zimmer was almost worse than having trained killers trailing her. The image of him, splotchy-faced and holding a gun as he rushed past Holden, would stay with her for a long time.

To think she once found Ned handsome. Tall and blonde with a face more suited to modeling than firearms, he attracted a lot of female attention. When he turned all of his considerable charm on her, she'd felt lucky. Special.

Little hints didn't come until later. He chose what she ordered in restaurants. He picked out her work wardrobe. Messages from friends never got to her. He moved her stuff into his apartment before she ever agreed to live together.

By the end she doubted her judgment and taste in men. Worse, she knew she couldn't continue as a therapist. No one wanted a pathetic victim of verbal abuse and emotional battering handing out relationship advice.

Holden shut the front door behind them and ran a hand through her hair. "You okay?"

His sweet concern nearly broke her. All the frustrations of the past few days bombarded her. Her muscles felt weak and jittery. If someone asked her to hold anything heavier than a pencil, she'd likely drop it. Strength abandoned her the second after they walked out of Holden's condo, leaving her embarrassing past sprawled right there on the floor.

She smiled up at Holden. "I will be."

"We'll get something to eat and then—" He looked past her into the dining room. "Vince?"

The new name had Mia spinning around. A man walked toward them with his hand outstretched and a genuine smile playing on his mouth. "Holden, how are you?"

"Let's just say it's been a long day."

Mia caught the quick glances the older man shot her. Gray hair with a tall and lanky runner's body. She pegged his age somewhere in his late fifties. That made him older than the Recovery agents, but he appeared fit. His intelligent green eyes didn't appear to miss much.

"What happened?" Luke asked Holden as he moved up behind his guest.

"I'll fill you in later."

Mia had to smile at Holden's dismissal. He acted as if it was normal to tackle an ex-policeman and then threaten to kill him.

"Who is… Wait a minute." Vince dropped Holden's hand and then moved to shake hers. "You look familiar."

Just what she needed—more people recognizing her from her boss's public lies. "I have one of those faces."

Holden laughed. "Nice try."

"People are looking for you," Vince said.

She liked the man's smile and the easy way he fit in with the rest of the house. "And that's a bad thing. Trust me."

"I do."

"Walters is ratcheting up the threats." Holden tightened his hand on her back.

"Meaning?" Luke asked.

"He sent someone with a message for Mia."

Vince shook his head. "That guy continues to be trouble."

She thought of her boss more as a criminal. "There's an understatement."

"What are you doing here?" Holden asked Vince.

"I called him. We came across some encrypted files Rod uploaded onto the secure server and not in the usual case section." Luke clapped a hand against Vince's shoulder. "Thought Vince could help us ferret it out."

"You're a computer expert?" The roles started to make sense to Mia. Though from what she could see of Adam, all six-foot-three of linebacker shoulders and bent over his laptop at the table, it looked as if he had the issue under control.

"No, I'm Rod's former partner."

"WitSec," Holden explained.

The acronym rolled around in her head until she deciphered it. "Witness Security Program?"

There was just no end to the complex pasts of these men. She figured them all for military-turned-agents of some sort. It looked as if their experiences, although all dangerous, were much more varied.

"We were U.S. Marshals before anything else. Rod left years ago, but I stayed."

"I still don't understand," Holden said.

"This came today." Luke handed Holden a large beige envelope.

"You opening my mail now?"

From his tone, Mia thought Holden was only half kidding. For a private man, and he was one, having someone dig through his personal papers would be a violation. He didn't seem to catch the irony of how a guy who investigated other people for a living hated being investigated.

It didn't matter if Holden was upset because Luke acted as if he had every right to dig into whatever he wanted. "If you have secrets you don't want me to see, don't bring them into my house."

"Fair enough." Holden opened the envelope and drew out the piece of paper inside.

Luke motioned for them to retire to the dining room. "Let's sit down."

"Where is everyone else?" she asked.

"Claire needed to pick up some stuff for the house."

"Luke made Zach and Caleb go with her," Adam said with a laugh.

That almost made her feel sorry for Claire. Mia couldn't imagine trying to buy milk with those two brutes hanging over her shoulders and glaring at anyone who got close. She slid into the seat next to Holden and watched him take out the single sheet of paper.

"Glenna Reynolds and Penny Wain." He flipped the paper around but there was nothing else on there. "Should those names mean something to me?"

Vince took the paper and repeated the names out loud. "They're two witnesses who were under our protection, mine and Rod's."

Interesting choice of verb tense, in Mia's view. "Were? As in used to be?"

Vince slid the document back across the table to Holden. "I'm retired. My old cases have been reassigned."

"Are these women in some kind of trouble?" Holden asked.

Vince shook his head. "I've checked with my sources and the women are fine."

"I haven't found anything to contradict that, though getting into the WitSec database is pretty near impossible," Adam said.

Vince frowned. "It should be totally impossible."

"Yeah, should be." Adam scanned the screen in front of him. "The encrypted files on Rod's computer have initials that match these ladies' names. I'm thinking that's not a coincidence."

"Would Rod have kept files on the women even though he no longer was responsible for their care?" Mia asked.

"I can answer that one." Holden hesitated only a second. "No."

She tried to put the pieces of his past together in her head. "Were you in—"

"No."

She stared at him, looking for signs he was covering, but his blank expression didn't give anything away. "I'll believe you."

He smiled. "That's good to hear."

She turned back to Adam. "Can't you break the code?"

At this point she assumed they could do anything. She couldn't imagine a bunch of computer language holding these guys back.

Adam didn't act offended. He kept tapping on the keys, barely looking up to acknowledge the other people in the room. "It's not anything I recognize, but I'm trying."

"Does this mean Rod is alive and hiding?" When all eyes turned in her direction, Mia's confidence stumbled. "What?"

"We're going on the assumption he's alive," Luke explained. "But, yes, he could have arranged to send this once he knew he was in trouble. The timing might not be proof of life."

The scowl on Holden's face let them all know what he thought of the topic. "More important, do these two women have a tie to Walters?"

"You know I can't give any personal information about people in the program." Vince cleared his throat. "But, no."

"This could be unrelated to Walters. It's possible that some part of the crap hitting us now can't be traced back to him. Kind of doubtful but still possible." Luke sounded as skeptical as she felt.

"I can't see a connection," Vince said.

"You think we have two unrelated apocalyptic problems happening at the same time?" Holden shook his head. "I don't buy it."

"Why?" Neither did she, but Mia wanted to hear his reasoning.

"Rod was poking around in WitSec and he's now missing. That's too much coincidence."

Vince cut Holden off. "But the hearings are about disbanding the Recovery Project. As far as I know, you guys haven't done any work with WitSec."

"True, but it's not that easy. Never is." Holden's hand rubbed up and down her back.

"We're racing along here assuming Walters was acting on a favor for the Samson brothers. That he's punishing Luke and Claire and taking us all along for the ride."

Mia hated thinking that she worked for a man whose priorities were so convoluted. She wasn't naive. She'd lived in the metro area since college. She understood how power could corrupt. But she hadn't seen it coming this time. Just another example of her poor read of the men in her life.

She looked up at the one man who struck her as the real thing. The same guy who touched her without thinking about it and made her wish for a few moments alone. "And?"

Holden shrugged. "I think there's more. A connection we're not seeing between Rod's side project and Walters's determination to destroy us."

Vince put his hands against the table and stood up. "You've convinced me. I'll do more digging."

"We'd appreciate it." Luke stood up and shook the older man's hand. "Let us know what you find. Hopefully, something."

Holden glanced at her and then back to Vince. "If you could also stay quiet about Mia."

"Understood."

Luke saw Vince to the door. "We're here and waiting."

The passive response surprised her. Once the front door closed, she leaned into Holden and whispered. "Are we actually waiting for someone else to gather information and feed it back here?"

He winked at her. "Of course not."

"Do you trust Vince?" She asked her question in a whisper, but when Adam smiled she knew he'd heard.

Holden took more than a few seconds to answer. "For the most part."

The man had trust issues. "That's not very positive."

"He was Rod's partner, not mine."

"So." Luke clapped his hands together as he walked back into the room. "What's the real plan?"

The words spilled out of Holden with a practiced ease. "Get into Walters's office and grab his private computer. If there's a connection to these women, it should be in there."

"He's likely moved it by now." Luke leaned down on his elbows against the back of a chair.

"I can check on that." Adam finally looked

up. "I'll ping it. Not as obvious as Holden's hacking, but it should work."

Holden ignored the joke. "A congressional office should be more secure than a regular house. I'm betting it's still there."

"Lots of security. Badges." Luke dropped his head between his hands. "I don't like it. It's not going to be easy to get in there. Even harder to get out without trouble. Frankly, we have enough problems without inviting more."

For smart guys, they were missing a simple solution. She waited until they all shared that we're-thinking-on-it look before she jumped in. "I'll get you inside."

Luke peeked up at her. "You're missing, remember?"

"I am betting you guys know how to create false credentials, yes?" She'd bet they could do much more than that but she wasn't sure she wanted the full rundown.

Adam's eyes narrowed. "It's probably better I don't answer that until I know your plan."

"I have a key to the office. We just have to get into the building downstairs and then bide our time until the place clears out. Then I can lead us into the Congressman's personal office."

"*Our* time?" The chill to Holden's voice could freeze meat.

"I'm going with you."

"No." Holden crossed his arms over his chest and leaned back far enough in his seat to make it creak. "Absolutely not."

"I work there. I have been to numerous hearings and events. I know how to get in and where to hide."

Holden pointed across the table. "Adam can figure it out. It's too dangerous for you to be there."

"As opposed to watching you fight with a police officer and then threaten to put a bullet in him?"

Luke shot up straight. "What?"

"It was nothing." Holden didn't even spare his friend a glance. His focus stayed right on her.

"Since you threatened Ned and gave him a message for Walters, I think we better move tonight. Before Walters starts deleting the trail to him." She smiled because she knew she had their joint attention now. She also knew she'd win this battle. "If there is one."

Holden shook his head. "I haven't agreed that you're going anywhere."

"Doesn't matter. It's happening."

Luke rapped his fist against the table. "Care to tell me about the police situation and these messages?"

Mia noticed Luke hadn't said no. The only impediment was Holden, and she could work around him without a problem. "You're going to be angry when Holden tells you what happened."

Luke exhaled. "No surprise there."

"Then would you be surprised if I told you the guy was my ex?"

Chapter Fourteen

The fake badges and her wig and glasses got them through the metal detectors on the bottom floor of the Rayburn House Office Building, where a significant number of high-ranking members of Congress worked surrounded by young and eager staff members. It was shortly past four and close to the time for official public lockdown for the night, but they got in.

More than three hours later, Holden tried to ignore how pleased Mia was that her plan to get them inside worked. He sat on a table and fought off the inevitable boredom that came from waiting.

Mia kept busy. Her high heels clicked against the floor in time to the spring in her step. She paced the small conference-room space waiting for the right time to move in.

And she did look good. The short navy skirt barely skimmed her knees. With each step it inched up higher and he wasn't the only one who noticed. A few of the men who'd passed by in the hall gave her legs a second look.

Now they were on the second floor on the back right side of the modified H-shaped building. Walters's office sat two stories up on the opposite side, facing the Mall. They picked this area thinking the distance away from Bram's private rooms would provide cover.

It proved to be the perfect hiding place while the public entrances shut down and the staffers filed out. To anyone watching on a security camera, they'd appear as nothing more than two staffers stealing a quiet minute alone. Interesting but not illegal.

His watch beeped and he glanced down at the screen. "It's time."

"A message from Adam?"

"He gave us the all clear."

"It's a little scary how much you guys know about what's happening in rooms you're not in."

To Holden complete intel was a necessary part of the job. Essential, actually. Being unprepared meant danger. With Mia along, he wasn't taking any chances.

"The goal is to have this run smoothly," he said.

"Of course."

"Up the stairs and into the office." He ran through the plan again. He ignored her when she rolled her eyes in response.

"We've been through this."

He kept thinking if they went through it one more time she'd have the steps memorized and all would be safe. But the way she frowned told him he'd only succeeded in annoying her. Tough. "We're doing it again."

"We're doing it again."

"Apparently."

"No strange movements or staring at the cameras. Head down and act normal and it will feel normal." He repeated the mantra to her two more times on the stairs.

When they hit the landing, Mia rounded on him and stuck a hand in his face. "Enough. I get it."

"We need to be prepared."

"I'm about to hit you."

"Then I guess you got it." He reached behind her and pulled the door to the hallway tight so she couldn't open it. "Let me check it out first."

"After you."

He pressed on the handle and opened it a slit. He saw a line of dark brown double doors leading down the hallway but no people. "All clear."

She led the way to the middle of the longest stretch and stopped. The plaque included a room number and Walters's name. The reference was to the eighth congressional district.

Just as Holden told her to do, she stayed calm. No shaking or panic. She slipped the key in and pushed the heavy door open. Except for a light on the receptionist's desk, the place was dark. Off to one side he could see a room full of cubicles. In front of them was a closed door to the Congressman's private office.

He lifted his finger to his lips and walked over to the room, nice and quiet. A soft knock and then he waited. When no one called out or came running, Holden turned the knob.

The room looked like he thought it would. Oversize desk. Oversize chair. It all matched Walters's oversize ego.

But no laptop. "Is the desktop an office computer?"

"Yes and he barely uses it."

Holden slipped the gloves out of his suit jacket pocket and handed a set to her. "Touch as little as possible but look through everything. Files, whatever it takes. We're looking for evidence that ties him to WitSec, or Recovery, or Rod. Got it?"

But she was already working. She opened the slim door to a small coat closet and started rifling through the boxes she found there.

He didn't waste any time either. He rolled out the file drawers and pawed through the files. They all had headings that referenced bills and committees and issues. He grabbed the employment folder with Mia's name on it and scanned for anything that might help.

Mia moved to the desk. Systematically, she poured through the stacks of paper and then targeted the drawers. Every one opened.

"We're doing this the wrong way." She delivered that opinion from behind Walters's desk.

"What do you mean?"

"He'd keep it in a locked place. In the evenings when I'd come in to take out the letters he'd signed, the laptop was here. Later it was gone."

Not the news Holden wanted to hear. "You think he takes it home at night?"

"I think he hides it. He's not the kind of man who would leave incriminating evidence just sitting around. He's also too lazy to drag a laptop around with him."

"Impressive guy. I can see why people voted for him." Holden kept his voice light, but on the inside the pressure started building.

The safety of a lot of people depended on him finding an answer. Not just the lives of his friends were at stake. They could fight back. The beautiful woman across from him was much more vulnerable. She'd been assaulted and threatened. If any single moment had played out a different way, even slight, she'd be dead. He'd never be able to live with that.

He wasn't a guy who shared his life, and no one should get stuck trying to sort out the nightmares that haunted him, but he wasn't ready to let her go yet. He definitely had to see her safely through this situation.

"Walters is the type who expects his staff to schlep everything," she said. "But he's not dumb. He wouldn't let someone who sits in a cubicle be responsible for carrying around something so important."

"I'm open to any ideas. Where do you suggest as the next place we look?"

She scanned the room, from the plush

carpet to the decorative dark wood squares on the wall below the chair rail. "A safe."

"Where?"

She pointed at the panels. "What's the chance one of those open?"

He followed her gaze. "Pretty good."

It made sense. A makeshift safe that passed for part of the wall. Nothing stuck out or looked different. Still, they'd tried everything else.

They hit the floor, both of them knocking and listening for a hollow echo. She started under the window behind the desk and went to the left. He picked the nearest square to his right.

The thumping kept time with the ticking grandfather clock in the corner. He'd tap. She'd tap. Before they knew it, they tapped a steady beat. Minutes passed without conversation or success.

Without warning, Holden's watch beeped. A third dot showed on his miniature schematic. It took a second for the information to process in his brain. That was just long enough to be dangerous.

He'd lost focus, hadn't seen the problem until it was on top of him.

"Who are you?" The voice came from the doorway.

Holden lost his balance and hit the wall. He turned in time to see a tall man step into the room carrying a stack of files. Confusion raced across the man's face as his stare bounced around the room.

Short hair and glasses and wearing a red-and-black-stripe tie Holden figured was a uniform because he saw it over and over again in the hallways since they entered the building. From his endless studying, Holden knew every detail of Walters's life, from his two teen kids to the ex-wife who lived in southern Virginia, outside the bustle of the city.

Holden recognized the man who walked in—couldn't remember the name but the face definitely looked familiar.

Holden stood up, sparing a glance at the desk. He thought that was the last place he saw Mia, but there was nothing there now. He hoped she dived under the furniture and stayed out of sight.

"Take it easy," Holden said as his mind flipped through possible ways out of this predicament.

He couldn't afford to be found here. He also didn't want to hurt this guy since his only offense, as far as Holden could tell, was a case of poor timing.

"How did you get in here?" The man took a step back.

Mia had warned Holden about the emergency assistance buttons hidden around the office. Other than the ones at the receptionist's desk and near Walters's chair, Holden had no idea where the other ones were. He wasn't about to let this guy get to one and call security. There were too many people in the room already.

"I was in here earlier this afternoon and lost my favorite pen." Holden held out his hands, trying to keep the other man calm.

"No, you weren't."

"We missed each other."

The guy's chest rose sharp enough to signal his difficulty in breathing. "I know the Congressman's schedule. You weren't on it."

Holden ran out of lame excuses. That left violence.

Before he could formulate a reasonable plan, Mia popped out of the closet, swiping a trophy of some sort off the credenza as she went. The guy must have heard her or felt the air shift. Just as he started to pivot, Mia swung the bronze statute in a wide arc. The corner connected with the man's head.

He went down in a whoosh. His body folded, as if every bone turned to liquid.

Holden reached the guy right as he crumpled in a heap on the carpet. "Damn, Mia."

"Oh, my God." She stood over them with a hand over her mouth and the weapon clenched in her hand.

Holden felt for a pulse. He saw blood but that wasn't unusual with a head wound. Blood didn't necessarily mean death or even a serious wound.

"It's David," she said in a voice thick and trembling.

"Who?"

"Walters's chief of staff. David is the man who hired me."

"We'll get him help, but we need to get out of here now."

"I can't…" She continued to stare, wide-eyed and horrified, at the man at her feet.

"Mia?" He snapped out the name to get her attention. "Finish looking for the laptop."

"What?"

"We still haven't found what we came here for. Check the last few blocks."

She pointed at the unmoving man on the floor next to Holden. "But, he—"

"I've got him. David will be fine." Holden nodded toward the far wall. "You go."

Something clicked because she went from pale and withdrawn to jumping around the room. On her knees, she gave a brisk knock to each of the remaining doors while Holden made sure the blood on David's head didn't signal a bigger problem.

The rapping sound stayed consistent until she reached the last panel. With her fingernails tucked in the seam, she pried open the door and revealed a safe.

"Here it is." She sounded unnaturally giddy, her voice high and breathy.

Holden poked around the injured man's pockets and found a handkerchief to hold to the wound. "Is there a lock?"

"Yes."

Walters made everything so difficult. "Switch places with me."

"I don't think so."

"We don't have time to argue about this."

Mia didn't move. "What if he wakes up? He'll recognize me."

She had a point but he was the only one in the room with safe-breaking skills. At least he thought that was the case. "Which is why we need to move fast."

Mia walked over, her feet dragging, and sat on the floor with David's head in her lap. She shrugged out of her jacket and pressed it against the wound.

"Just do whatever you're going to do. Fast." Concern and more than a little guilt floated around her.

Holden reached into his pocket and took out a small packet. The putty stuck to the wrapper but finally came loose. The guard downstairs let it pass. Holden didn't blame him. Zach had devised the paper packaging to look like gum. In reality it was a concentrated explosive device.

Hardly an expert at demolition, Holden tried to both rush and be careful at the same time with the dangerous substance. The instructions were clear: push the sides together to ignite, then stick to the surface.

"Holden." Her voice cracked.

"What?" he asked without looking up.

"He's waking up."

David's feet shifted and he started to moan.

"Keep him still," Holden ordered.

"How exactly do I do that?" The words rushed out of her.

Holden tried to block it all out. He folded the material, then rolled over to her, ducking her head under his arm and covering her body with his. He heard a small hiss and then the bang akin to slamming a microwave door. By the time Holden sat up again, David's eyelids were flickering.

They'd just run out of time.

Holden crawled on his knees, waving away the puff of smoke and acrid stink of sulfur. Ignoring the heat, he reached in and picked out the contents of the safe. One laptop and a stack of papers. Tucking it all under his arm, he pushed to his feet and ran for the door.

As David's head moved from one side to the other and his hands pushed Mia's helping arms off of him, Holden hurdled over him. He reached down and scooped Mia off the floor, dragging her with him as they made their escape. He slowed only when they got to the front door to the hall.

"Head down and move to the stairs as fast as possible without running." The plan B formed as he walked.

"What happened to acting natural?"

"Security is going to study these tapes. We want to make sure we can't be identified."

They double-timed it back to their escape route. Despite the suit and stuff in his hand, he jogged. They hit the lobby without any trouble.

"Keep moving." He hustled her across the marble floor. When they got to the last corner before the lobby, they stopped and, while pretending to talk, checked out the trail to freedom.

The guard stood by the metal detector but everything appeared normal.

Mia tugged on his tie. "We need to go before David wakes up enough and calls for help."

Holden agreed. With his hand on her elbow and a fake smile plastered on his face, he guided her to the exit. Her head stayed down as she pretended to cough. He waved. They sailed through.

The second after they pushed the door, the speaker attached to the guard's shoulder squawked. Holden didn't wait to see what was happening. They ran down the steps and right into the car Caleb had waiting in the street.

Only then did he glance up. Instead of

swarming the car, the security appeared to run deeper into the building.

This time, Holden knew his luck held.

Chapter Fifteen

It took another three hours to quiet down the Hathaway household. Between the questions and the yelling, Mia had a headache.

Not that she blamed Luke for being furious with the implementation and potential fallout from the evening. Injuring a congressional staffer had not been part of the plan. It didn't help that Holden appeared determined to blame Adam for David slipping into the room unnoticed.

Mia knew the truth. She originally thought Holden was so closed and hard to read. But after spending time with him she saw every emotion as he felt it. He thrived on control and hated his lapse in concentration. The warning came and went and he missed it until it was too late.

And he hadn't stopped kicking his butt since. The frustration came out in fights with

Adam and arguments with Luke. In stomping around and a raised voice.

To Mia, it was transparent. Holden kept poking and pushing because he knew he could. They'd support him and that made his outbursts safe.

"I understand why you cut out down there," Holden said as he walked into the bedroom and locked the door behind him.

This was the second time he came into the room intending to sleep with her. The last was about protection and ended with him watching over her while she recuperated from her head injury. This time his purpose was equally clear.

Every other night, he fell asleep downstairs on the couch with work piled on his stomach. She found him there each morning. They never talked about the sleeping arrangements. They just fell out each night with him making the decision and her waiting in bed to see if she'd spend the night alone.

Unbuttoning his sleeves now, he stripped as he went. The trail led from the door to the dresser. A shirt draped over a chair and shoes abandoned on the floor behind him. By the time he got to the chest of drawers, he wore only a white T-shirt and pants.

She sat on the bed cross-legged and watched it all. Even with something as mundane as undressing, he commanded the room. His steps didn't falter and his self-assurance never slipped.

It was as if it never dawned on him that she might turn him away tonight. Not that she was going to, but he acted as if this was any other night. As if they hadn't committed a federal crime or hurt a man for simply doing his job.

Mia understood the guilt because she felt it, too. It lived inside her, growing and thriving despite the good prognosis for the man who trusted her enough to hire her.

"David is fine." She said it because she needed to say it and even though Holden already knew.

He dropped his gun on the nightstand like a man on a mission. "He'll be sore but okay."

"It's the mental damage I'm worried about."

Holden stared at her in the mirror in front of him. "From what I can tell, he's a strong guy."

Adam relayed the information about David's injuries earlier after breaking into hospital records and following the case on the police scanner. The story hadn't hit the news, but it would soon. This wasn't the sort of thing even Walters could hide. Not after all these government services and departments got involved.

Sure, Walters would downplay it. Refer to a breech or an accident. He'd insist security held and the guards did their jobs—the usual political speak that meant nothing and hid the truth.

She used to believe all that garbage. After everything she'd seen with Holden, she viewed all of those stories and political speeches differently.

But none of that changed what happened to David. He had a superficial head wound and no understanding of what happened to him. He remembered seeing someone and then getting hit. The lack of a story would make Walters's false one easier to create.

Mia blew out a relieved breath David was alive. When he went down, her stomach had turned and tossed. Her fingers had gone numb and her mind refused to tie her action to the obvious reaction. Being tracked and attacked was one thing. Launching an offensive strike on an innocent man made her sick.

She'd thrown up twice and showered once since coming upstairs. She'd wanted to crawl into bed, throw the covers over her head and forget the day. Instead, she settled for the subtle comfort of soft sweats.

Exhaustion pulled at her, but she doubted she'd be able to sleep. Her body tingled with unspent energy. And Holden's refusal to treat the moment as anything other than a normal night had her temper skyrocketing.

"I'm the one who hit him," she said.

Holden finally turned to her. "I know."

"His injuries are my responsibility, not yours. The plan was mine. The hit was mine. You can let yourself off the hook."

Holden eyes narrowed. "Are you okay?"

Hearing the concern, the fight seeped right out of her. "Not really."

"You did what you had to do."

"Does that make it all right?"

He slumped down on the bed next to her, exhaling as he went. He slipped his fingers through hers. "Sometimes innocent people get caught in the middle."

"That's a rough justification."

"I'm thinking that's the rationale Walters used to get the group disbanded. He doesn't like the consequences. Maybe that's valid."

"I didn't mean that. Walters is doing what he's doing for his own ends. Whether it's to help Steve Samson or pump up his ego, it doesn't matter. He's not you. I get that."

"I wish I could tell you the job is easy and always goes the way you think it will. It doesn't." Holden rubbed a finger over her knuckles. "But sometimes that's the best part."

"How do you figure that?"

"I didn't expect you to come flying through my wall and right up to my couch."

She gave him an exaggerated sigh. "That again. You just can't let it go."

Instead of laughing her comment off, he grew more serious. "I certainly didn't expect to feel what I feel for you."

Her heart bounced. Actually did a twirl and landed again. "What do you feel?"

"I don't honestly know."

She wanted more. "There are some obvious choices. Hate, frustration, distaste…any of those?"

"You know none of those fit."

He refused to break down that last wall. She wanted to kick through it. Push it over.

"Then tell me, Holden. Put it into words."

He went with the pure male choice. "I'd rather show you."

His arms went around her and dragged her

down to the bed. Her back hit the mattress as his body slipped over hers. From chest to knees, he covered her. His body heat penetrated her clothes and seeped into her chilled bones.

Hands traveled over her while his mouth pressed against hers in a kiss so deep it wiped out every thought in her head. Lips and fingers, an erection pressing against her hips. All that mattered in that moment was Holden and the tightening inside her.

She wanted him naked and inside her. Her hands stripped off his shirt and then reached for his pants. Tossing and shifting, she worked him out of his clothes and threw them on the floor. Her palms met with bare skin, smooth and burning hot.

His fingers were just as eager. They pressed against her breasts, caressing and exciting until the air punched through the walls of her lungs. The other hand moved over her, peeling her sweats off as he went. Skimming against her panties before dragging them down her legs.

Frenzied minutes later, they were naked and rolling across the bed. They landed at the bottom with his chest rubbing over hers. He nibbled his way down her neck as his hands drifted even lower.

He touched her then. Moved in soft circles that brought her hips straining off the bed. The heat inside her coiled, pulling all her muscles tight.

"Condom." She whispered the word as her arms fell to the side next to her head.

"I'll be right back."

Instead of lifting up, he slid over her, igniting her nerve endings with the friction of his skin against hers. That fast he was gone and returned. The fumbling in the nightstand only lasted a second.

A small rip echoed through the room as his hand returned to her lower body. His fingers brushed her softness, back and forth until her body clenched.

She pulled him over her. "Now, Holden."

He shifted against her, inside, filling her as the words stumbled off her tongue. "Yes."

Then he was moving.

Their bodies fell into a rhythm, a gentle push and pull that grew more insistent with each thrust. He went deeper, harder, touching off the fiery release inside her. Heat plowed through her as her heart pumped a frantic beat.

When his shoulders stiffened, she knew he hovered on the edge of pleasure. She tightened her legs around his waist and brought him closer to her. His release rocked them both. The bed creaked and their breathing mixed and thundered.

When sleep finally overtook her, she welcomed it.

HOLDEN FINALLY RELAXED. All the tension drained out of his muscles. Tonight, after the debacle with David, Holden couldn't control the adrenaline rushing through him. The energy bounced around inside, knocking and pinging against every organ. Just when he thought he could contain the explosion long enough to tame it by refocusing it into anger against Adam, Mia left the room. She said a courteous good-night, then started up the stairs.

Seeing her slim hips swish from side to side did him in. The spinning through his blood kicked up again until all he could think about was getting to her. He counted to ten three times and took a walk around the property before heading up the steps after her. It took all his will and concentration not to jump on her as soon as he opened the bedroom door.

She wrecked him. She took his ordered life with few emotional ties and ripped it all to hell.

He'd lived every day of his life since the time in the cave a certain way: on the edge and without being obligated to anyone. He stayed detached. He vowed to avoid any situation where he'd have to watch the life pump out of someone he cared about.

Not again.

He made an exception for the Recovery team not because he wanted to but because it just happened. Then he added Claire to his small circle because she bulldozed into his life through her love for Luke, and Holden couldn't shut her out.

But he didn't think he could bring Mia into the mix. A voice in his head warned that losing her would be the final deathblow.

Balancing one arm behind his head, he pulled her tighter to his body with the other. They could have these moments. This was about banishing fear and loneliness. About wiping away the sadness that moved into her eyes as David hit the floor.

In that second, in the dark room, she brought him peace. He wasn't a man who knew much peace.

"You're thinking loud enough to keep me awake." She mumbled the observation against his chest.

"Is that even possible?"

"Apparently."

He smiled because he couldn't help but feel good around her. "Just basking in the afterglow."

She looked up at him. "Man, please tell me that's not your best line."

"That bad?"

"Terrible."

"Tell me why you stopped being a therapist." He didn't even know the question hovered in the back of his mind until he said it out loud.

She frowned. "That's what you want to talk about after sex?"

He wanted more sex, but he knew this topic was too important to ignore. "I think so."

"I have to tell you I didn't see you as the type to want to talk about my background."

"Why?"

"Because I get the feeling you could find whatever information you wanted without any help from me."

He had checked on some parts, but this was different. This had to do with the private thoughts that couldn't be ferreted out in an online search. "Maybe I want to hear you say it."

She sighed. "Honestly? I left because I wasn't smart enough to stay away from Ned."

Holden wasn't expecting that. Zimmer didn't deserve that level of power over her or anyone. "What does he have to do with helping other people?"

"I couldn't save myself, so I was hardly qualified to save others."

Holden slipped his fingers through her soft hair because he wanted to touch her. "Are you kidding?"

"No."

"So, this is about punishing yourself."

"Not at all."

"That's what I heard."

"You're analyzing instead of listening." She swung her leg behind her as she balanced her chin on her hands and looked up at him. "Speaking of that, why are you afraid of tight spaces?"

He opened the emotional door and couldn't exactly blame her for pushing through. Or for wanting to know more about the man lying naked beneath her.

He deserved this. Still, it took two full minutes before he could get out the simplest of sentences. "Because I got trapped in a cave-in in Afghanistan."

"Sounds horrifying."

"That's pretty accurate."

"And?" She smoothed her hand over his chest.

"What?"

"I might not be practicing now, but the counseling skills are still there. I know when a person is evading."

"Have I ever told you how much I hate therapy?"

"Not a surprise, but that's not going to stop this conversation, so keep talking."

Minutes ticked by until the silence surrounded him. She didn't pry or insist. She just lay on top of him, looking at him with a calm reassurance that sucked away the rest of his resistance.

"The two men with me died. One immediately." When he closed his eyes he could see the blood spurt and the light fade out of the young kid from Kentucky. Twenty and fresh from combat training. The kid deserved better. "The other took longer to bleed out."

"You couldn't save them."

"Zach and the others dug from the outside. I shoveled through the dirt with my bare hands to try to break through." That same sense of helplessness washed over Holden now. "We ran out of time."

She ran her hand over his chest. "I'm sorry."

"Me, too."

She pressed her warm cheek against his skin. "I'm amazed you could go into that tunnel under your house at all."

If she had fired questions at him, he likely would have shut down. Instead, she remained silent. The supportive quiet gave him the will to keep talking, to spill his most private thoughts and biggest failings. "I'd been practicing, going down a few steps at a time to see what I could handle."

"Not a surprise either."

"Meaning?" He felt her smile against him.

"I can't imagine you coming up against anything you couldn't conquer."

Despite the faith and soothing talk, the conversation made him twitchy. He didn't want to dissect his feelings or get stuck in an impromptu therapy session. He didn't want counseling from her. Not at all.

"Speaking of conquering." He let his hand wander down to cup her backside in his palm.

"Wow, that's a gutsy comment."

"I have another condom."

"You're evading."

If she kept throwing out psychology terms, his plans would be shot. Nothing destroyed the mood for him quite like that. "Is that a no?"

She glanced up, her gaze wandering over his face before she smiled. "Did you hear a no?"

"I'm not sure."

"It's a yes."

Then her lips moved to his stomach and traveled down, and they didn't need conversation.

Chapter Sixteen

Holden left Mia in bed early the next morning and headed downstairs. With his muscles revived and his brain cleared, he was ready to comb through Rod's records and put an end to the madness. He wanted more nights like that with her, and that was only going to happen if the darkness hanging over their heads cleared.

He rounded the bottom of the stairs and realized he wasn't the only one up and functioning before seven. Adam and Caleb beat him to the pile of documents. They'd divided it and started working.

They sat on opposite sides of Luke's dining table with a pot of coffee stationed between them. Heads down and papers shuffling, they worked. Adam frowned at his computer monitor. Caleb tapped a pen fast enough to launch it into space.

"Gentlemen," Holden said in greeting.

"I know what we're doing here. Why are you here?" Caleb asked.

"I can work when I have to."

Adam snorted. "I'm not sure why you'd want to when you have a woman who looks like that upstairs in your bed."

Bed. Mia. Yeah, if his mind wandered there Holden would be running up the steps. "The only way she's going to be safe and we're going to find Rod is to jump on this."

Caleb tapped his pen against his teeth and glanced at Adam. "He struck out with Mia."

Adam nodded. "Definitely."

"I'm not playing, so don't even try." But Holden sure was tempted to set them straight. If he were a different guy and Mia meant less, he might engage in locker-room talk. But he was well past the age where that sort of openness held any appeal. "So, what do we know?"

"There's nothing about Glenna Reynolds or Penny Wain on Walters's computer." Adam pushed back from the table and folded his arms behind his head. "He tried to clear the hard drive but was about as effective with technology as you two would be."

"Meaning?" Holden asked.

"He has documents pertaining to the Samson trial and a file on each of us."

After breaking into a congressional office, Holden was hoping for something more. "We expected all that."

Caleb flipped through some pages and checked his notes. "He also contacted the Marshal Service. Did it under the guise of needing information about their policies and procedures for a funding issue."

Like a man of his position wouldn't send a staffer out in search of that information. Holden didn't buy the interest as genuine. "Sounds like garbage."

"Didn't get him anywhere, either." Adam smiled as if he liked the idea. "But I'm still digging."

"We have a bigger problem." Caleb talked to Adam but pointed at Holden with the tip of his pen. "Tell him."

"Got a red flag on our names. Looks like Walters is subpoenaing all of us to testify."

Holden dropped into the chair next to Caleb. "He's too stuck on our team. Rod ticked someone off. Someone high up with a lot of power and a few too many secrets, if I had to guess."

"Agreed." Adam nodded. "And no news on

Rod either. None of the usual signs tripped. Nothing on credit cards or banking. Nothing on the back channels or our private system. If he's out there, he's moving on cash and not leaving a trail."

"Which means he doesn't want us to know where he is or what he's doing," Caleb said.

Which meant there were only so many strings left to pull. Holden knew his range was limited. He wasn't the tech guy like Adam, or the demolition expert like Zach, or the forensics guy like Caleb.

Holden excelled at tactics and strategy. He needed to act like it. "Is David Brennan back at work?"

Adam glanced over at Caleb then back to Holden. "If I say no and I'm wrong are you going to crawl up my—"

"Sorry about that. I just didn't want any surprises when Mia was with me."

"Understood. I wasn't any happier about the unexpected guest. Believe me." Adam pulled in close to the table and typed for a few seconds. "And David is still in the hospital."

"So, now what?" Caleb asked.

The plan clicked together in Holden's head. Flushing Walters out might be the only solution. Get him worried and he'd make a mistake. Give him a target and he might misfire.

"Without David there to ID me, I think I should pay Walters a visit," he said.

Adam's smile doubled in size. "I don't know what you're thinking, but I like it so far."

"Is Walters scheduled to be in the office today or is he pretending to be too upset about his chief of staff to go to work?"

More tapping before Adam answered. "He's in."

"Put me on his calendar this morning. Make it look as if I was always supposed to be there. List me as some lobbyist or bigwig he'd be compelled to see. We'll do a bait and switch."

Caleb shook his head and smiled at the same time. "Luke is never going to go for this."

Holden had an easy solution for that. "We're not going to tell him."

"And Mia?" Adam asked.

That was one was harder. Holden glanced toward the stairs. "Her either."

LESS THAN THREE HOURS later Holden still thought the plan made sense. He sat on the love seat in Walters's waiting area and ignored the commotion around him. Staffers came in and out. The phones rang every few minutes, sometimes two and three lines at a time. More than once the receptionist commented on David and thanked the caller for the concern.

Ten minutes after the allotted appointment start time, Bram Walters strolled into his office. He read the newspaper and sipped his coffee. Not exactly the appropriate level of concern for a man who had his office broken into the night before.

Holden just waited for Walters to notice him.

The receptionist handed him a schedule. "Mr. Leonard is here."

The older man turned around, a huge smile plastered on his mouth. "I didn't see…"

If the sudden quiet was any indication, the offensive strike worked. Holden stood up, enjoying the win in this first battle. It was the ongoing war that worried him.

"I believe we have an appointment," he said.

The Congressman didn't show an ounce of surprise. "Leonard, is it?"

"Yes."

"Sir?" The receptionist kept looking

between the two men in front of her. "Is something wrong?"

The Congressman snapped right into campaign mode. "Of course not."

He motioned for Holden to precede him into the office. As soon as his office door closed behind them, Walters's welcoming pretense fell. An angry wash cleared his expression. Gone was the affable politician ready to schmooze a constituent.

He slid into his big leather chair. "I'm not sure this is a wise choice on your part, Mr. Price."

"Why?" Holden didn't wait for an invitation to sit. He took the chair closest to the desk and glanced around, looking for evidence of the break-in. Overnight, everything had been fixed. It sure did pay to be in charge.

"You probably haven't received it yet, but you're under subpoena to appear before my subcommittee. Very soon, in fact," Bram said.

"I find it hard to believe you don't have anything better to do than to drag us all in to answer the same questions." Holden took in the photos on the wall and books lining the shelves on either side of the window. "Isn't there a ribbon cutting or luncheon you could go to?"

"I didn't put you in this position."

"Feels like it."

"Your boss didn't show for his testimony yesterday." Walters didn't sound upset by the slight. "If Mr. Lehman plans to avoid his responsibility, then the obligation falls to all of you."

"What do you think you're going to find?"

"The truth."

This guy wouldn't know truth if it walked up and smacked him. "Clearly you wanted my attention, Walters."

"That's Congressman Walters."

Holden chose to ignore the ego shove. "You have it."

"This isn't about you." The Congressman's chair creaked as he leaned back.

"I find that hard to believe."

"It's about an agency being funded without congressional oversight."

A nice bit of doublespeak. Looked as if the man had said the phrase so often he now believed it. "Then get angry with the agency and the people who gave us the money. They're the ones who cut you out of the process. They owe you the explanation."

"Then there's the problem with how you operate. It's about all of you working outside the law."

"Give me an example."

"Hacking into private computer systems." Bram glanced at the space that used to house his safe. "Breaking into offices."

There was no mistaking those references. The Congressman knew who was coming after him.

Good.

"You don't like that we catch criminals?" Holden asked. "I'd be careful with that sentiment at election time. The way I hear it, voters don't much like bureaucrats who are soft on crime."

The other man never ruffled. Holden kept poking, jabbing at his ego. Everyone had a soft spot. Holden knew Walters wouldn't be any different.

"I'm referring to the Samson debacle," Walters said.

The case that blew their cover. Holden wouldn't change anything because they saved Claire and the horrors of those days bound Luke and Claire together, but the ramifications kept cropping up. Luke suffered a debilitating shoulder injury. Even now he didn't have full use of his arm. The team lost its office and privacy and its leader.

"I think we see that one differently."

"How so?"

"Your rich friends committed fraud and murder. Phil set up his ex-wife, Claire, and then tried to kill her." Just listing the sins of the Samson brothers brought a new flush of fury over Holden. "Now you're covering for his brother, Steve, who was in on it the entire time."

"I am investigating tactics."

"Don't you worry you're hitching your reputation to the wrong star?"

Bram's blank stare faltered. "Your team blew up a house and left a trail of bodies across my congressional district."

"We caught an embezzler and killer."

"We'll see what happens at trial."

"Is that what this is about? You want to discredit us to mitigate the impact of the testimony against Steve."

"Of course not."

"How much of a campaign contribution did Steve Samson give you?" Holden traced the lettering on the Congressman's embossed nameplate at the edge of the desk.

"My campaign finances are a matter of public record."

"What about the nonmoney contributions?"

"Such as?"

"Admittedly you're not hiding behind your mother's skirt, but you are hiding behind your brother's company. Using his men to fight your battles." Holden straightened the nameplate as he made a tsk-tsking sound calculated to drive the other man nuts. "I'm not aware of any sort of congressional immunity that will protect you from murder charges."

"Those are serious accusations." Bram dug his fingers into the smooth leather of the armrests.

"You started this fight. Did you honestly think you could push my team without us shoving back?"

"We're done here." The other man stood up.

Holden refused to stand up. Not when sitting down would tweak a man like Bram Walters. "Did you get my message from Ned Zimmer?"

A dull red appeared on Bram's cheeks. "I don't know what you're talking about."

"Mia is off-limits."

His expression changed then. It was unreadable, but the mere mention of her name touched a nerve. "If you're referring to my employee, I'm very concerned about her well-being."

"Then stop trying to kill her."

"I'm a member of the House of Representatives."

"That only means you have the most to lose."

Bram's hand inched toward his phone. "Are you threatening me, Mr. Price?"

This time Holden stood up. "Merely pointing out that if we found the information on the Samson brothers and used it to take them down, we'll find something on you."

"You have five seconds to leave or I'll call security."

"No, you won't, but I'm going." Holden took a few steps and then slowly turned around, drawing out the tension as much as possible. "You know, it's funny, but I swear I've been in here before."

Bram fumed. "Never again."

"We'll see."

Chapter Seventeen

Bram called his brother the second Holden Price left his office. In the hour it took for Trevor to pull away from his meeting and get to the office, Bram's rage had morphed into an unruly beast.

He started down this road because Steve Samson asked for a favor. Then Bram received inside information on the Recovery Project's operating strategy and he saw an opening— establish his position in the intelligence community and help Steve. But the inside source turned to blackmail and Trevor stepped in. Everything blew up right after.

Between poking around in WitSec and fighting off the Recovery members, Bram had sunk deep. Commandos staging home raids in the suburbs and people breaking into his office. A simple favor had spun out of control. Instead of earning political capital, Bram now stood on the brink of losing everything.

Trevor walked into the office without bothering to knock. "I do not appreciate being summoned to your office."

"Holden Price was here."

"You told me that much already in your message." Trevor stopped in front of the desk. "So?"

"He knows everything."

"I doubt that."

"He made it quite clear I'm his target." And Bram didn't like having a bull's-eye on his chest. He'd always done everything the party wanted. Voted the right way. Kept his public persona clean. Even had a good relationship with his ex-wife to prevent any scandal.

He still didn't understand how he'd gone from that place to an accomplice to murder. He hadn't made the call or asked for the help, but all the death unfolding around him came from Trevor looking to get rid of his ex and ending up dragging them into a WitSec cover-up. That made it Bram's responsibility.

"It would appear it's time we got rid of Mia Landers and her boyfriend." Trevor spelled out his newest violent plan with the same emotion he used to order breakfast.

"I told you no more killing. I never signed up for that." Bram struggled to reconcile the man Trevor had become with the one he used to be. Power and money corrupted. Bram knew that, but this time they went one step further and destroyed a conscience.

"Don't be naive," Trevor said.

Bram despised the way his brother talked down to him. No other person in the world dared to do that. "Excuse me?"

"What did you think would happen when you drove Mia out into the woods? Even if she'd admitted working behind your back, what would you have done?"

"The goal was to scare her."

"No." Trevor shook his head. "You knew that eventually I would step in and take care of her."

Bram refused to believe that was true. He never wanted death. Never. "I didn't think it would come to this."

"There is only one way for this to end. You've laid the groundwork for discrediting the Recovery Project. Now we need to take care of the individual members before they uncover the WitSec issue."

"That's a bit obvious, don't you think?"

"I would think it's preferable to losing your office and being indicted."

Something inside Bram shriveled. Sitting

there, staring into his brother's cold eyes, Bram knew the truth. If this all became public, Trevor would be fine. He had a backup plan of some sort. He'd come through without losing a thing.

And he'd make sure Bram didn't.

MIA STORMED AROUND the Hathaway family room. She'd never been this angry. And not for her. This wasn't about Holden leaving the bed before dawn or not sharing his plans. A little after-sex talking would have been nice, but she was a big girl.

She understood Holden's intimacy meter was out of whack. She could deal with that. It was the other that had her shaking with fury. This was about his disregard for his own safety. About his idiocy in picking a fight with her boss.

She stopped pacing in front of the fireplace and aimed her finger at Holden's chest. "You made yourself a target."

The man didn't even flinch. He acted as if it was perfectly normal to walk into a congressional office and issue threats. "We have to bring this thing to a close."

"That's your excuse?"

"It's the truth."

"Walters could have had you arrested."

Holden shot her a you've-lost-your-mind glare. "For what?"

This was on purpose. He understood the significance of his actions but pretended otherwise. She couldn't find any other explanation for his cluelessness. "You're impossible."

"You're no prize today either."

Holden acted so sure of himself when he came home a half hour earlier. He practically vibrated with excitement over the situation he had created. The lack of self-preservation scared her. She'd seen it before with trauma victims. They rushed in and took foolish risks because they just didn't care about the consequences anymore. They functioned as machines.

She needed for him to stay human, with all the feelings and fears of any normal person. For him. For her. For them.

Maybe he thrived on action and always would. That wasn't unusual for a man in his profession. She could learn to handle that. Claire had. But courting death, begging for it, was a different thing.

Thinking about Holden rushing to his death scraped Mia's stomach raw. Not seeing him, not being with him. Those options took away every ounce of strength she'd regained since leaving Ned.

She loved Holden. Somewhere, somehow, she'd started believing in a man again. Not just any man. In Holden. Watching him throw all that away without even a second thought crushed her.

"Why are you so angry?" Holden asked with a stunned little-boy look that suggested he really didn't know.

Yeah, he wasn't ready to hear about her feelings. Rather than send him running into more danger as he tried to get away from her, she tamped down on her needs, burying them deep, and focused on common sense. "You are forcing the issue by daring Bram Walters to kill you."

"Rod is missing." Clearly Holden thought that explained everything.

"I get that."

"He could be running out of time."

An excuse. Rescuing Rod was only part of the plan here. She felt that with a rock-solid surety inside. "That is not what this argument is about and you know it."

The confusion cleared from Holden's face. Every muscle stiffened and his mouth pulled tight. "Don't do that therapist crap and try to read my mind."

"I'm not."

"Sure as hell feels like it."

She refused to get sucked into his insecurities on this issue. One of them needed to stay rational and on topic. "You're acting as if your life doesn't matter."

"I'm doing my job."

"You are risking your life. That is guilt talking. Guilt and despair and post-traumatic stress disorder."

The tension building around them exploded. The quiet turned heated as the air pulsed.

"Do not diagnose me." His fury grew and flailed around unleashed. If he talked any louder, the entire household would come running.

She was surprised they didn't have an audience already, but she knew the others could hear. His voice boomed to the rafters.

"I am trying to talk some sense into you," she said in the calmest voice she could muster.

"You are trying to control me."

The oxygen sucked right out of the room. "What is that supposed to mean?"

"You know."

"Hey." Luke picked that minute to poke his head in the doorway, knocked on the wall. "Sorry to interrupt."

Holden didn't even spare him a glance. "Not now."

"Yeah, the timing isn't great, but we have an emergency." Luke glanced around as if trying to figure out if they'd broken any furniture during the fight.

That quick, the tension snapped. All the anger swirling around them evaporated as they focused on the third party in the room.

"What's the problem at this hour?" They'd been in a constant state of readiness since she arrived. She guessed this was an escalation of some sort.

Luke looked back and forth between Mia and Holden. "Someone is trying to hack into our security system again. Thanks to Adam's tinkering, everything is holding, but it looks like we might get a second wave of intruders this evening."

Holden did this. He went to the Congressman and now his brother was sending in the troops.

She rounded on him. "Are you happy?"

Holden blinked a few times. "Actually, yes."

"It's okay. We'll be prepared for them this time," Luke said.

Boys and their war games. The fighting and disregard for danger made her head pound. It made her shaky with fear. "You are not in a war zone. This is a house in the middle of a neighborhood. A place with kids across the street."

"We know," Holden said.

"Then you understand that you just dragged danger right to Luke's door."

"We'll be ready," Holden said, repeating Luke's empty promise.

Nothing she said broke through. If Holden wouldn't listen to her, maybe he'd listen to a friend. Someone he did trust, because she clearly was not that person. No matter how much she wanted to be.

She glanced at Luke. "You deal with his death wish. I'm done."

LUKE AND HOLDEN WATCHED her stalk out of the room. The banging of her feet against the stairs highlighted her anger.

As if Holden needed another reminder.

"You okay?" Luke asked.

"Obviously, I'm doing great. Totally in control of my life at the moment." Holden leaned back on the sofa and balanced his head against the cushion.

"Is she right?"

He closed his eyes. Maybe if he blocked them all out the discussion would go away. "Not you, too."

"She's concerned. Some guys would take that as a good sign. It means she cares."

Holden refused to deal with that. He could barely take care of himself. He couldn't take her on, as well. Opening up meant dealing with the good and the bad, letting her dissect and try to fix. He wasn't ready.

"She's trying to diagnose and cure me. I've had more than enough of that over the past few years."

"You lived through hell. I'd worry if you didn't get some help."

"I can do my work and get through the day. That's enough."

Holden didn't open his eyes, but he felt Luke's stare. Heard the footsteps and crunch of paper as he sat down on the magazines on the coffee table.

"I know what it's like to feel like there's nothing left." All the heat had left Luke's voice.

"Don't."

"When Claire walked out on me and married someone else, I went a little crazy."

Holden opened his eyes. "You got her back."

"Not before a lot of self-destructive behavior." Luke stared at his hands before looking back up. "I'm just saying you can play this thing another way."

"How so?"

"You have a reason to look to the future now."

The only thing that interested Holden less than a life talk with Mia was one with Luke. "What are you talking about?"

"Mia."

He wasn't ready to go there. Holden wondered if he ever would be. "No."

"Think about it."

Mia was all Holden thought about. He had no idea when she started to matter that much, when he began planning his life around her, but the promise and potential for failure paralyzed him.

Luke exhaled. "In the meantime, you need to get out of here."

"Why?"

"We're ready for whatever comes through

the door, but I want everyone downstairs as a precaution tonight."

Holden heard what Luke didn't say—underground in the windowless room. The claustrophobia. "I'll be okay."

"Adam says the chatter is just about this house. You should go to your condo and wait it out."

Running away from a fight. Holden had never operated that way and didn't intend to start. "I'm not leaving you guys to battle without me. Besides, it could be a trick."

"Maybe, but nothing is going to happen here if I can help it, and there's no reason to put your head through the pressures of being trapped downstairs."

"I don't like it."

"Me either." Luke cleared his throat. "You could have told us about the spaces thing, you know."

All of a sudden everyone was a therapist. "I'm handling it."

"You sure?"

"Definitely."

Luke started to say something and then stopped. "Okay."

"I still don't like the plan for tonight."

"Think positively. You can take Mia out of the potential firing line."

"But strand the rest of you?" Holden shook his head. "No, thanks."

"For once, think about what you need. From what I can see, that means Mia."

Chapter Eighteen

Mia's anger still burned bright later that evening. She'd been given a thin protective vest, rushed out of the house and dragged into town by Holden. He'd said as few words as possible. She only knew they were going to the condo when they pulled into the underground garage.

Watching him now, she questioned the intelligence of taking him away from his team. He paced around in front of the kitchenette like a rabid animal. His shoulders were rigid and his mind far away from here.

She understood the anxiety. He hated being left behind. To a man like Holden that meant weakness.

And he was driving her crazy. The constant movement and mumbling to himself. The lack of conversation and deadly quiet. Her nerves jumped every time he turned a corner and started walking back to the door again.

His watch beeped. "Here we go."

She was at his side within seconds. "What?"

"Huh." Holden tapped a few buttons. "That's odd. It's a text from Adam."

"So?"

"It's not our usual mode of communicating."

"He said he had to make adjustments because of whatever jamming devices Trevor's men used."

"True."

"What does he say?"

Holden reach for his coat. "They need us to come back."

"Why?"

"The communication system isn't holding as Adam had hoped. He isn't getting a good feed and they're not sure where the intruders are." Holden slipped the jacket over the shirt and vest. "I need to play lookout from outside the house."

More danger and he rushes in without thinking about it. If he didn't care about his safety, she would. "No."

"Mia."

"What if it's a trap?"

"Then I still need to go."

"It's too dangerous."

His teeth snapped together. "I'm not that guy."

"Which?"

"The one who sits back and lets everyone else do the work."

The truth of his comments hit her. This wasn't just about taking unnecessary risks. This spoke to a bone-deep need to rescue. He played the hero even as he insisted he wasn't one. It was natural to him.

It terrified her. But that was her issue. Her place of vulnerability. If she loved him, she had to accept who he was underneath.

"I'm not staying here alone," she said.

The crisscrossing lines in his forehead disappeared. "No, you're not."

"ANYTHING?" LUKE TORE his attention away from the flat-screen monitor. They were deep underground, but picked up a satellite signal without trouble.

Adam shook his head. "All's quiet. No movement by the outside gate. No one trying to break down the door."

"Isn't that good news?" Claire asked from her position at the head of the large conference table.

They hadn't finished off the walls or floors,

but they'd managed to drag furniture down there. The technology was in place. Computers, a server, file cabinets. The equipment lined the one cement wall by the stairs. The others consisted of mud and studs where walls would eventually be erected.

It was dank and musty. The lights cast some light but not enough. It was the perfect place to hide.

Caleb shifted in his chair. "It's too quiet."

Luke rubbed his face. "Okay, let's not panic. Maybe we misinterpreted the chatter."

Adam scrolled through the data. "There was a tactical assault planned."

"This feels wrong." Zach hit the remote and changed the image on the screen to different shots of the yard. "Like a setup."

"What's happening with Holden?" Luke asked.

"Nothing."

Luke came away from the wall to stare at the computer monitor over Adam's shoulder. "What does that mean?"

"His signal hasn't wavered." Adam pointed at the schematic. "He's in his condo. They both are. Their signals are coming through clear."

Luke took some satisfaction from that news. "At least something is working right."

"Wait." Adam leaned in closer.

"What?"

"The signal just bounced. I went from a clean screen to an empty one."

Claire rushed over as the men crowded around Adam. "What does that mean?"

Adam shook his head. "Could mean nothing."

"Or?" Luke asked.

"We've been getting a false signal. They aren't in the condo at all. They're moving." Adam looked up. "And they're not alone."

HOLDEN DIDN'T NEED to be told about the potential danger. He sensed a trap. Instead of heading down the elevator to the underground garage, they used the stairs. No chance of the doors opening and an armed gunman being right there in front of him ready to shoot this way.

But no matter how much he rubbed the back of his neck, the feeling of danger wouldn't go away. He could smell it all around him, felt it push down on him from above and close in from the sides.

He hid his anxiety from Mia. As she

grabbed on to the back of his jacket, he tried to hold his body still. No shaking or panic. For her he'd be calm. He'd stay focused.

"Are you ready to tell me what's wrong?" She whispered the question right into his ear.

So much for believing he was fooling her. "I think the scare back at the house was a diversion."

"You mean that we're the target."

She didn't miss much. He kind of wished she was a different type of woman at the moment, one who couldn't see the disaster looming. "Yeah."

"They're after us."

"Whoever 'they' are."

She tugged on his shirt and shifted positions. "We should go back upstairs."

They couldn't slow down or go back. He guided her back to the step above him. "You keep moving. First rule of combat. If you hesitate or stop, you're an easy target."

"The garage won't bother you?"

For once, the reference to his weakness didn't tick him off. He didn't have time. "It's not closed in. The bigger problem is who might be in there waiting for us."

"That's not very comforting."

He squeezed her hand and met with ice-cold fingers. "I know."

"Did you call the team?"

"Can't get through. The signal changed about halfway down, which makes me think we've been working from a fake one."

He looked at his cell. Still no signal there either. That one had nothing to do with Trevor's men. It was an unfortunate side effect of the building.

She blew out a harsh breath. "Could the news get worse?"

"Things can always be worse." He believed that. Lived by it. "My car is the second on the right as we enter the garage. I'm going to open the stairwell door and you're going to run as fast as you can to it."

She nodded but didn't say a word.

"Head down and don't look back." He pressed the extra ignition key in her palm. "If I don't get in right behind you, you drive away."

"No."

"This isn't the time to argue. I need you out of here. Drive as fast as you can." He put his cell in her hand and folded her fingers around it. "Forget about the phone blackout.

The concerns about communication are gone. You call Luke as soon as you get a signal."

"What are you going to do?"

"Get you in that car and then get you out of here." He couldn't look into her terrified eyes for one more second. "On the count of three. I'll stay high. You go low."

He pushed the door open, letting it slam against the far wall before it knocked back against him. The smell of gasoline overwhelmed him. A wall of blackness loomed in front of him. Someone had cut the lights.

Mia crouched down and took off for the car. She grabbed the door handle and then fumbled for the key when it didn't immediately open.

He kept watch. He swung the gun around, taking in every inch of the one-story garage. At least the spaces he could see. He took two steps and was surprised when the sound didn't echo back to him. Footsteps didn't sound in the distance.

Maybe they were alone, but it seemed too easy.

Still skeptical but not one to question luck when it sprang up in front of him, Holden headed for the car. His shoulders stayed tense and ready. With his finger rested on the trigger, he rounded the back end. A small burst of relief hit him when Mia slipped into the passenger seat. But he didn't let up. He kept his gun trained and his knees bent.

The slight scrape of cloth against cement registered right before his foot hit something on the ground. Looking down, he saw Ned Zimmer's face staring back up, gun raised and a triumphant smile on his face.

Something flashed. Blasts thundered, echoing through the cement-lined space. Burning heat raced down Holden's arm as his body pushed back and his head shot forward. He could almost hear his spine snap.

Then he hit the hard ground, bouncing first on his lower back and then slamming his head. His vision blurred even as the sound of Mia's screams registered behind him. He inhaled as deep as possible, trying to force oxygen into his body and wake up his dead limbs.

The sole of a foot passed in front of him. He didn't feel anything, but his body jerked and Mia cried out. If only he could open his eyes, move his arm.

Suddenly a face hovered right above Holden's. Not Mia's face. This one belonged to Zimmer.

"You should have killed me when you had the chance," he said.

Holden tried to open his mouth, to say something. Then a blinding pain seared through his skull and the world went dark.

Chapter Nineteen

Mia tried to move her arms. Her shoulders ached from being pulled behind her and her throat hurt from screaming. Seeing Holden get shot, watching him go down like that, left her feeling battered and bruised. Ned should have hit and kicked her because she felt every shot Holden suffered. She would have taken each hit if he could have been spared.

Stuffed in the trunk of a car, listening to the road bumps beneath her head, she had too much time to think. The image of Holden's lifeless body kept playing in her head. His eyes rolled back. His body folded.

She'd heard about heartbreak but never experienced the actual sensation of having her chest physically ripped in two. Now she had. Every part of her thumped with pain. Her bones ached and stomach kept rolling. Even her hair hurt.

She knew she needed to focus if she had

any hope of living through the next few minutes, but her mind kept flashing to Holden. He had sensed the danger and put his body in front of hers.

When the car rolled to a stop, she listened for familiar sounds. Mostly she tried to figure out how to kick the crap out of Ned when he opened the trunk. One good whack might give her a minute to run.

The door flew open and a flashlight shined in her eyes. She could smell the outdoors, the scent of pine and fresh earth. The brisk night air blew across her cheek as sun left its last streaks across the gray night sky.

Something else tickled her senses—the faint odor of burning wood.

"There's someone who wants to talk to you," Ned said as he grabbed her arms and yanked her to a sitting position.

That fast, she lost any advantage. "Don't do this."

"I was paid to bring you here. That's what I'm doing."

"No." He reached for her but she shrank back, trying to make her body smaller, and struggled out of striking distance.

"That's enough." A dark coat moved into her line of vision. "Take her out of the car."

Congressman Walters. She'd recognize the measly voice anywhere. What she once took for strength she now tagged as out-of-control ego. He thought he could do anything and get away with it.

When she went to yell, Ned stuffed a rag in her mouth. She kicked and thrashed, trying as hard as possible to inflict damage. But she was no match for his strength. He outweighed her by more than fifty pounds and his grip crushed her bones. He had her out of the car and on her feet within seconds.

The Congressman stared at her, hate showing on every line of his face. Gone was the elder statesman who won awards for constituent service. He could attend every breakfast at every elder home in the county for the rest of his life and he'd never wipe the stain off of him. He'd turned into a vicious madman.

"You have caused me a serious amount of trouble."

She couldn't answer. She wanted to spit on his perfectly shined shoes.

"Now you're going to tell me what I need to know." Bram glanced at Zimmer. "And your ex-boyfriend here is going to help me."

HOLDEN GRABBED FOR the door and tried to pull his upper body off the ground. His hand smacked against the metal and slid back down. The jolt sent pain ricocheting inside him.

None of that mattered.

He had to get to Mia. He lost track of time. He thought only a few minutes had passed since Zimmer took her away, but he wasn't sure.

Concentrating, he threw his arm up in the air again. This time his fingers snagged the handle. Ignoring the creaking of his bones and knocking inside his head, he lifted his body off the floor.

The throbbing started in his fingers and increased in intensity until it reached his lungs. With a groan of frustration, he gave a final shove up to his knees. From there he crawled up the car to his feet. Just as he lost balance, he pivoted and threw his weight until he sprawled on his stomach on the hood.

The sound of his heavy breathing drowned out everything but the screech of tires behind him. Thinking a second attack wave was on the way, he reached for his gun but couldn't find it. He had a knife by his ankle but didn't think he could get back up again if he bent over.

"Holden!"

The voice sounded familiar but he couldn't

place it. Footsteps pounded and then Caleb and Adam were on top of him, touching and talking to him. None of it penetrated Holden's brain.

Adam rolled Holden over and ripped open his jacket. "There's blood." Adam's harsh tone matched the look on his face.

"It's okay. One of the shots got under the vest. It's not serious." Caleb dumped his medical bag on the car next to Holden's head.

He heard the clink of metal and the conversation above him.

"Then what has him dazed?" Adam asked.

"Something else."

Holden's surroundings finally registered. He grabbed for Caleb's shirt. "He has Mia."

Caleb's hands never stopped moving. "Who?"

"Zimmer."

Caleb swore before he regained control. "Not to worry. Zach hid a transmitter on his car and we can follow it via satellite. We can find her."

"Luke?" Holden asked.

"He's back at the house making sure this wasn't part of a two-pronged attack." Adam nodded to Caleb. "We'll get you there and get you some help."

"First we have to fix you up enough to travel," Caleb said as he pulled the thread and bandages out of his bag.

Holden didn't feel any of the medical care. "No time. Have to go after Mia."

With a light touch Caleb pushed Holden's shoulder back against the car. "You can't even stand up."

"The shots hitting the vest knocked me out, took my breath."

"Are you bleeding anywhere else?

"Cracked my head against the cement."

"You've got a knot back there already." Adam felt along Holden's hairline.

The touch shot in his head like a sledge-hammer. He bit back the bile rushing up his throat. If he threw up, Caleb would take him to a hospital. With his mind clearing, Holden knew they couldn't waste hours, even minutes, on that.

"Doesn't matter." He struggled to sit up and the garage spun around him. "I brought Mia into this. I left the trail from her to me."

Caleb helped Holden balance on the car. "Don't do this now, Holden."

"We're going to find her. And I'm going to need your help." As much as it killed him to say it, he knew it was true. "I can't do it on my own."

"How?" Adam asked.

Holden knew he only had one option. "You drive. Caleb, work on me in the car."

MIA SAT ON THE SAME STACK of branches Holden had used to hide his car. She recognized the area around what used to be Holden's cabin. With the extra light, the sights and sounds of the woods came back to her.

She used to think of trees as peaceful. Thanks to Bram Walters, they now reminded her of death. There had been so much in this area. All of it traceable to the man standing in front of her.

But there were benefits to being in a place she knew and they didn't. Not far away was the entrance to the underground cavern she'd used to escape once before. She wondered if it had collapsed in the explosion. The part she could see remained intact, which meant it might be usable.

"Why are we here?" she asked, pretending not to know.

Bram looked around, clearly pleased with this part of his plan. "Seemed poetic to bring you back here."

"You mean that no one will think to look for me here."

"Your only ties to this place are through Holden Price and I understand that he is no longer with us." The Congressman looked over her shoulder to Zimmer for verification and received a head nod in return. "There you go."

She couldn't let her mind go there. She had to believe Holden survived, that somehow the thin vest blocked a gunshot. She prayed he was on his way now, guns blazing with the entire Recovery team riding behind him. More than that, she willed him to be alive.

"Tell me how much Holden Price knows." The amusement had left Bram's voice.

She didn't even understand the question. None of them understood the larger scheme behind the Congressman's actions. Admitting that would only hasten her death. She needed time.

"Everything," she said.

He didn't even flinch. "I think you're bluffing."

"Then we're even because I think you're disgusting."

Ned backhanded her across the face. "Show some respect."

Bram held up his hand, looking every inch the proper statesman in his dark business suit. "That's enough, Zimmer. We don't hit women."

"Right," she scoffed. "You just kill them."

Bram's head fell to the side. "I'm not going to kill you, Mia. Why would I do that?"

"To save your own a—?"

"The language isn't necessary."

She stared from the Congressman to her ex. "Oh, I see. You're going to have your hired dog do it for you."

Ned shifted closer to her, but Bram called him back with a firm shake of his head. "Whatever Officer Zimmer—"

"*Former* officer," she pointed out.

"Decides to do with you after I'm gone is not my business."

The possibilities ran through her mind. Air clogged in her throat at the thought of Ned touching her again. "You can't be serious."

"I'm here to ask a few questions only."

Mia looked at her boss, tried to read him but couldn't. "You actually believe that don't you? You think you can separate out your sins like that. Launch an attack and then not take any responsibility for the results."

The Congressman frowned. "The only thing

I've done is look into a law-enforcement group about which I received a complaint. That is my job as a sitting member of Congress."

She really wanted to throw up on him. "Spare me."

"I did my job."

"You tried to protect Steve Samson, an accused murderer."

The comment had Ned looking at Walters. Ned had many faults. Because of his need for complete submission and obedience, he was a woman's worst nightmare. But he lived by the badge and hated the idea of criminals going free.

His black-and-white view of crime had led him to commit a few offenses of his own, but he never saw it that way. If he had to beat out a confession or bend the truth to make a conviction stick, he did it. In his world, the accused didn't have rights, didn't deserve them.

Mia knew she could use Ned's warped sense of justice against him. "You've been feeding Steve Samson's attorney information and helping to get him off."

Ned's eyes narrowed to tiny slits. "Is that true?"

The Congressman pretended to wipe something off his sleeve. "Of course not."

"Yes, it is." She focused all of her energy on riling Ned up. "Why do you think he hates the Recovery Project team so much? They caught his friend and put him in jail."

Bram held up his hand. "The source of my information about Recovery doesn't matter since the information was correct."

Ned took a step closer to Walters. She doubted the Congressman saw it or that it even registered he might be losing his muscle's loyalty.

"What about WitSec?" she asked, hoping to hit on that piece of information that would make her former boss slip.

His face closed up. "I don't know what you're talking about."

"Rod Lehman. Glenna Reynolds and Penny Wain." She continued to shift her wrists behind her. The rope cut into her flesh and warmth she knew to be blood spread over her fingers, but she kept pulling.

Ned was facing Walters now. "Who are those people?"

"None of your business," the Congressman snapped.

The rope wouldn't give no matter how hard she pulled, and she had to be careful there or risk letting Ned know what she was doing.

"The good Congressman, your new boss, is involved in some nasty stuff, Ned. The kind of thing you hate."

"What is she talking about?"

Bram finally focused on Ned. He screwed up his lips and shot him a look of disdain, as if Ned was nothing more than filth. "Why are you listening to her?"

"She seems pretty sure of her facts."

"You idiot, she's trying to upset you."

And she was doing a good job. Mia could see it on Ned's face. He'd moved to judgment. He was assessing Bram Walters and finding him wanting. Once Ned made that turn, there was no going back.

"Tell me about WitSec." Ned aimed the gun at Bram.

Panic flared in the Congressman's eyes for the first time since they had walked into the woods. "You idiot, you work for me."

"I'd stop with the name-calling if I were you. Your power doesn't extend out here."

As the men argued, Mia looked around. She could make it to the rock entrance, but they'd see her and track her. She could run through the woods, but without transportation or hands to steady her body, she'd be at a significant disadvantage. She needed a miracle.

A twig crunched behind her. Heat brushed against her back. She could feel knees near her shoulders. She inhaled, trying to detect Holden's familiar scent but she couldn't. Every cell inside her willed Holden to walk out of the woods and touch her.

"Put the weapon down, Zimmer," Caleb ordered.

Wrong man.

A rush of questions screamed to get out. She hoped that Caleb's presence meant Holden was nearby, that he had survived and called for help.

Fear lingered, too. Him being here might mean Holden couldn't. She tried to stand, to grab on to Caleb and beg him for answers, but her legs wouldn't move.

At the sound of Caleb's voice, Zimmer swung around. Bram followed a beat behind. Both men looked stunned to find someone else deep in the woods.

"Who the hell are you?" Zimmer asked.

"He's one of the Recovery agents." The Congressman didn't look so smug now.

"Caleb Mattern." He shifted to stand beside her. Caleb helped her to her feet and handed her a pocketknife to break through the rope. "Put the gun down, Zimmer. Walters, hands up."

"That's Congressman to you."

"Not for much longer."

"How did you find us?" she whispered. It wasn't the question she wanted to ask, but it was the only one she could force out.

"We've been following Zimmer ever since he came after you at the condo."

Caleb didn't use Holden's name. Didn't reassure her he was okay.

All the pain she'd been pushing from her mind crashed right into her heart. She assumed she'd know if he was dead. She'd feel it run through her like a sword. Instead, her body went numb.

Bram swore under his breath. "Idiot. You led him right to us."

Zimmer turned to Walters, not trying to hide the wild anger now. "I'm not going to jail over you."

"You each have a gun." The Congressman pointed at Caleb. "You're probably a better shot, so shoot him."

Like a dream, the rock opened and Adam stepped out. He came right out of the passage, but it looked as if he rose from out of nothing. "We have two guns."

The Congressman went pale. "What the—"

"I'm not telling you again, Zimmer." Caleb didn't move. "Gun on the ground."

"No, not like this." Zimmer looked around at the other men.

Mia knew that face, knew that last drop of desperation. Her ex was a narcissist with an overinflated sense of self. He was the type who would try to shoot his way out of a situation rather than go to prison. That fall from public grace would be too much.

"Caleb, be careful," she whispered.

He put a hand on her shoulder. "We're good."

Zimmer acted like a hunted animal now. He looked around as if trying to find a means to escape. "I am not going to prison."

"Yes, you are." The deep voice had them all turning.

She heard Holden's voice and searched the horizon until she found him. She took in his battered face, then felt a hand push her to the ground. In a blur, she saw Holden move from behind the trees just as Caleb threw his body over her. Shots rang out through the woods. Dirt kicked up around her. Footsteps pounded. She heard shouts and a scream of fury.

A loud thump rumbled the ground in front of her. When she looked up, she saw the

Congressman's body right beside her, blood pouring out of his mouth and staining his shirt.

In another glance she watched Ned raise his gun in her direction and Holden shift his stance. A final shot blasted around her, then nothing. Silence fell over them.

It was a few more seconds before anyone said anything.

"All clear." Caleb shouted the words.

She didn't wait for him to move. She shoved him off and ran to the area she last saw Holden. He knelt on the ground next to Ned's lifeless body with a gun still in his hand. Holden leaned back on his heels, his chest rising and falling on heavy breaths.

Seeing his faraway stare was all that stopped her from plowing into him. That and Adam's firm hand. "Whoa."

"Holden." She approached him slowly, watching his gaze adjust to her being there.

"You're okay." Holden repeated the phrase four more times before his shoulders slumped.

"Holden?"

"He'll be fine." Adam put his body under Holden's arm and lifted him to his feet.

She couldn't help it. She ran her hands

over his chest, looking for injuries. When she pulled a palm back, red stained her fingers. "He's bleeding."

Caleb wrapped an arm around her shoulder. "Not from this."

As if she cared about the timing. "Help him!"

Adam nodded. "We will."

"Mia." Holden reached out and ran his limp fingers down her cheek. "Don't know how, but love you."

Then he passed out.

Chapter Twenty

Holden stood next to the bed in Luke's upstairs bedroom and tried to fight off the numbness in his limbs.

This wasn't about the injuries. This was about the dragging in his head. He tried to put his thoughts together and understand all that had happened over the past few days, but his mind couldn't grasp it.

They barely knew each other. There was no way Mia could have come to mean so much in such a short amount of time. It didn't make sense.

In so many ways, they were wrong for each other. She liked to dissect actions and talk about feelings. He wanted to hide away and deal only with what was in front of him. That's all he could handle.

But he wanted her. Every day and all the time. He turned to her when he woke and looked for her at the end of every hard moment. She made life better.

Seeing her in danger had sent a shot of energy ripping through him, wiped out all the pain and the knocking in his head. He had to get to her and destroy anyone who touched her. The emotions were raw and uncontrolled. For the first time in his life, he couldn't hold back and hide his fears. They raged around him.

He didn't know what they had, how she felt, but he wanted more. He knew, in her eyes, he was a broken man. Years before he walked into a cave a strong man and walked out too scared to go into a small space without breaking into a cold sweat. That wasn't the kind of man a woman needed.

He opened the dresser drawer and then slammed it shut again, letting the hard bang vibrate through him.

A decent man would let her go, but he couldn't do it. What ran through his mind were schemes and plans to bind her closer to him. If he could keep her there, he could work on being a better man. They could make love and he could heal. Eventually, maybe, she could learn to view him as something more than a potential client for her therapy practice.

And, yeah, he'd have to learn to deal with that, too. He'd grind his teeth and keep his mouth shut. Whatever it took to have a chance with her, he'd do. No matter the sacrifice or personal toll, he'd make it work.

He knew what a good woman could do for a man. He'd seen it with Luke and Claire. Holden craved that closeness, that connection. The chance his life could mean something again, that he could beat back the nightmares that haunted him, made the risk worthwhile.

Problem was he loved her. It surprised him, stunned him, but the crushing feeling wasn't going away. If anything, it kept growing until it took over everything else.

Her. Them. Together. He had to figure out a way to make it work. Start with sex and build. He was a strategy man and he'd make this one work.

MIA WALKED INTO the bedroom she'd been sharing with Holden expecting to find him asleep, or at least resting. She'd settle for seeing him sitting down.

He was standing at the dresser, fiddling with something in the drawer. He had to lean one hand against the top to stay upright. Even then he looked crooked, with his shoulders dropped on one side and his body weight supported on one leg.

"What do you think you're doing?" she asked.

When he looked up into the mirror and watched her close the door, a sexy smile edged the corner of his mouth. "Standing."

"Funny man."

"I've been lying down for hours."

"Hour. One hour. Actually, more like thirty-five minutes." She held up the fingers to highlight her point.

"I feel fine."

He looked ready to fall over.

"I don't believe that for a second." She stopped beside him and glanced down to see what he found so important. Condoms.

When she looked at him again, he had the nerve to wiggle his eyebrows. "Well?"

"You've got to be kidding."

"No."

"You banged your head and sprained a wrist. You have broken ribs, and don't tell me they don't hurt because mine are only bruised and they're sore."

"My lower half works fine."

She wasn't sure what was going on. The man professed love to her in the minutes before he fell over and now was obsessed with sex. This was not a normal reaction. She'd been through the textbooks and had never seen this.

She thought about having Adam check Holden for a head injury. "You are going back to bed."

"That fits in with my plans."

She turned him toward the mattress and grabbed the condoms out of his clenched fist. "Lie down."

"Yes, ma'am."

She threw the packets over her shoulder and as far away from him as possible. "Not going to happen."

"You sure?"

Man, he was tempting. "Absolutely."

He frowned up at her like a sad little boy. "Killjoy."

Maybe, but she noticed that as soon as his back hit the mattress, his eyes went shut on a sigh. He leaned his head against the pillows and slowed his breathing.

Exhaustion and pain. She knew the signs.

They'd rushed him back to the house so Caleb could administer aid. She tried to get Holden back in the car and to the hospital but he yelled loud enough to wake the neighbors in the next county.

He fought them on everything and insisted he was fine. Tried to wipe the blood away and cover the winces when he moved.

The man had lost his mind. "Sex? Really?"

He made a face. "We work well together in bed."

That was male code for something. She wasn't sure for what.

"Tell me what's really going on here." She stood over him and tangled her fingers with his.

"Nothing."

"I'm not leaving until you say."

He smiled. "That's not the incentive you think it is."

"Holden."

His eyes opened as his lips went flat. The blues focused on the ceiling instead of her. "I almost lost you."

Then she got it. *Men.* Sex was a way of connecting. He was trying to reinforce the bonds. Women went for words. Men loosened a bra.

She crawled in next to him and let out a little sigh when he wrapped his good arm around her. "You saved me."

"If Adam and Caleb hadn't been there…" He rubbed his eyes with his palm.

Guilt was kicking his butt. She knew him well enough to know the injuries took something from him. He had to be in control and handle every situation just right. Having her taken away from him in that garage pushed something inside of him.

It was an unrealistic burden for anyone. Holden just refused to see that.

She sat up so that her mouth hovered right over his. Before she could say anything, he leaned up and kissed her. Not a hot kiss moving toward passion. This was tender and loving.

All at once she understood what was really happening here. He was a man who had experienced unspeakable tragedy in the past and closed off his heart. In the woods tonight, in the heat of danger, he opened his soul again. He told her he loved her. She'd been full of hope ever since.

She smoothed her hand down his T-shirt. "Do you remember what you said to me before you passed out?"

He stayed quiet for the longest time. She was about to ask again when she felt a small shift underneath her.

"Yes." His simple word came out strong and clear.

Without looking up, she knew he was staring at her. "Why does it scare you so badly?"

"You can't turn off the psychologist, can you?" It wasn't delivered with his usual scathing tone whenever he got to the topic. The words sounded more like a conclusion.

She sat up and balanced her upper body over him with an arm on either side of his chest. "It's who I am."

"Then why aren't you practicing right now?"

The memory of Ned's face came rushing back. Holden had killed him. One shot and Ned went down. She knew Ned didn't deserve her pity or remorse. Still, the idea that someone she once cared about, who played such a large role in who she was, was gone left her chilled from the inside out.

"I explained that. My instincts were off. I knew that after the Ned situation."

"That's an excuse."

She was about to deny it, then stopped herself. "I guess that's true."

"You're tougher than you give yourself credit for."

She kissed Holden on the nose. "You're not so bad yourself."

His palm brushed up and down her arm. "I'm serious."

"I can see that."

"You're letting Ned have a hold over you."

"I've moved on."

"Then don't let him take your career. If you want to do therapy, do it."

The idea sounded so easy. Maybe he did steal more than her pride and self-esteem. Maybe she let him take something bigger. For the first time in months, it also sounded appealing. She missed the one-on-one with patients. She made a difference to a few people. Losing that had taken a part of her.

"Maybe."

Holden shrugged. Actually blushed a little. "You can always do profiling for the team. You know, keep the skills fresh."

The thought made her smile. "Can you see working with me every day?"

"Yes."

The possibilities spread out in front of her. All those doors that had closed creaked back open. She wasn't ready to push them and walk through or even knock, but the world wasn't as shut off and impossible as it had been when she drove that car through Holden's front door.

He gave her that. He never judged her decisions or doubted her. He listened, protected, enticed and now loved.

She'd never been so grateful for a car accident.

"I love you." She rubbed her finger over his lips.

Those blue eyes bulged. "What?"

"I know that scares you." Though she didn't see the panic she expected. "You've hidden yourself away for so long that you might not even know that someone could love you, but I do. I didn't plan it or see it coming until it was too late."

"Mia…"

She pressed her fingers against his mouth. Now that she wanted to say it, she *wanted* to say it. "I won't diagnose you or try to change you, but I do want to spend my life loving you. All you have to do is give me a chance."

He moved her hand. "Yes."

It was her turn to sputter. "What?"

The sparkle returned to his eyes. "I think that was a pretty clear answer."

Her brain malfunctioned. "You said yes?"

"I meant the words when I said them to

you out there in the woods, Mia. I mean them now." His gaze searched hers, all evidence of a haze now gone. "I know it all moved too fast, but I'll mean it forever."

Her mind refused to process. The news was amazing, the best, but she couldn't get from the fear she expected from him to the point where everything fell into place. "You mean you…"

"I love you."

Tears pushed against the back of her eyes. "No fears or worries about being tied down?"

"Lots of worries but none of them about being stuck with you. Thinking about a life with you is easy. I'm the question mark here."

"Not for me."

"Almost losing you made everything click." He wiped the wetness away from her cheek. "A few weeks ago I would have stood in those woods and focused on how I couldn't rush into that cave to save you. I would have been frozen, beaten myself up and gotten sucked down into this paralyzing vortex. You would have paid for my arrogance and failure."

She knew all of that without him telling her,

but the fact he could share his fears opened up a lifetime of hope for her. "Now?"

"You matter more. I focused on what you needed instead of what I couldn't do and let Caleb and Adam be the bigger heroes."

"You were pretty heroic out there, too."

"I drew up a plan that ignored my ego." He shook his head. "Don't get me wrong, if I had to walk in that tunnel in order to save you and have the element of surprise, I would have figured out how. But I didn't want to take the risk. Not with your life. Not when I didn't have to except to stroke my own ego."

Sunshine burst to life inside her. She felt full. Bathed in a love that would sustain and complete her. "You are a good man."

"All I want to be is your man."

"I thought I'd have to wait forever for you to see it."

He kissed her, light and gentle. "I'm slow but not stupid."

"Good to know."

"I'd rather have a few weeks with you than a lifetime of wondering what could have been."

"That's very poetic." She leaned down and kissed him back. No hesitating or sweetness. This was a kiss meant to claim.

When they broke apart, they were both breathing heavily.

He rested his forehead against hers. "You bring out that side of me. You take all the dark parts and flood them with light."

She'd never heard anything so romantic. Never felt so adored and respected. With Holden she wouldn't have to fear or choose her words. They'd fight, make love and live.

His shoulders stiffened. "You know I'm talking about the whole thing, right?"

Saying the words still proved to be a battle for him, but she wasn't about to let him back down now. *"Thing?"*

"A future. Whatever we can figure out and make work, I want it."

She'd never get a more heartfelt declaration of love and commitment. For Holden to mention any of those, to want all of them, showed how much he'd changed.

"I want that, too."

He relaxed back into the mattress. "Perfect."

She fell against his chest and inhaled his clean scent. She could lie there forever, but she doubted she'd be able to keep him down for long. He was determined to get up and get back to work.

"I have one more question for you," he said as he ran her fingers through his fingers.

She couldn't imagine what else was bouncing around in that head of his. "What?"

"Any idea where you threw those condoms?"

She laughed. "You have a one-track mind."

"That's about right."

But he wasn't the only one who wanted the intimacy. She'd count down the days until he was strong and healthy enough to run his hands over her again. "I'll make a deal with you."

"What?"

"You rest and I'll tell you how much I love you."

"I like it so far."

She nuzzled his ear with her nose. "Then I'll tell you all the things I plan to do to you once you heal."

"Deal."

"THEN WE HAVE an understanding?"

Luke stood at his front door. He had a gun tucked against his back and the doorknob in his hand. "You can leave my house."

Trevor turned the folder in his hands end over end. "I need to know we've reached an agreement of sorts."

"Fine. You spin your tale about your brother. In return, the investigation on the Recovery Project and hounding of its members will stop."

The other man smiled. "A good decision since you don't have any evidence against Bram anyway."

"He kidnapped Mia." That piece still grated on Luke. He knew Trevor was involved in all of this and he was going to skate.

"My understanding is that Ned Zimmer, a former lover, did that."

"Then there's the part where Bram really died in a shoot-out and not rushing to save Mia from Zimmer." Luke wondered how many people Trevor had to pay off to make that sorry story fly.

"And I'm sure you wouldn't want your agents implicated in a well-respected public official's death."

Luke refused to risk any of his men. And that's how he thought of them. His men. "We understand each other just fine. So long as

Steve Samson goes to prison and never bothers my wife again, I'll ignore your brother's hand in trying to free a killer."

"You sure you don't want to throw in with me? All of your men could do quite well and would benefit from my payroll."

Luke couldn't think of a more despicable idea. "You ready to tell me what Bram was really doing, other than the Samson deal, and where Rod Lehman is?"

Then there were all the questions about WitSec and why Trevor risked his men on Bram's stupidity.

"I have no idea what you're talking about," Trevor said with a smile that telegraphed the opposite.

Liar. "Then we're done."

"I'll trust you to honor our deal based on a conversation. No need for cumbersome paperwork."

"Yes." Luke opened the door and hit the button for the far gate. "But, Trevor. This is a onetime agreement. If I find evidence about Rod or anything else and it leads back to you or your business, I'm coming after you."

"I assure you that won't happen."

"And if you come near my house or my people again, I'll kill you."

Trevor tipped his head. "If you'll excuse me, I have to go plan a funeral."

Chapter Twenty-One

One Week Later...

Luke and Holden stared at the man across the conference-room table. Being called into Bram Walters's former office didn't sit right with Holden. The Congressman had just been buried. With full honors, of course. Fellow members stood on the House floor and spoke of the man's contributions and the sad news of his heroic death. The newspeople declared him a great legislator lost too early. Even his ex-wife cried.

No one mentioned the fact he was a criminal because only his brother, Trevor, and the Recovery team were alive to tell those secrets.

Holden refused to give Bram Walters another minute of his time. They'd agreed to provide cover for him. Until they drew out the person pulling the WitSec strings and found Rod, nothing else mattered.

Trevor could handle his mess with his men and explain their losses. Holden didn't know their identities and the evidence to those crimes was long gone. Trevor made sure of that.

"You're telling us you're running for Walters's seat?" Holden shoved aside the glass with the official congressional seal.

David Brennan folded his hands in front of him. "I've been asked by the party to consider filling his seat. It's not as simple as being appointed by the governor. There will be a special election."

Luke snorted. "I'm hoping you're better at the job than your former boss."

David's smile slipped. "He was an exemplary legislator."

"I'd settle for an honest one." *Or one who didn't kill,* Holden added in his head.

"I've talked with several members of the subcommittee." David shot two folders across the table. "There's a general consensus that Representative Walters may have let personal concerns get in the way of his sound judgment with regard to the Recovery Project."

Holden opened the cover but didn't bother

to read the contents. "Keep talking like that and you'll make the perfect politician."

"Steve Samson will no longer be receiving help from powerful friends."

"Good to know." Holden glanced at Luke and saw his friend's jaw tighten at the mention of Samson.

"Having said that, Representative Walters wasn't the only member with concerns about your work and the lack of oversight from any governmental entity."

"We figured that out," Luke said in a dry tone.

David just kept talking. "However, people are realistic. It's an unsafe world, one that requires individuals with specific skills. Your skills."

Holden wanted to go home to Mia even if it was to his dreary condo. With her it was brighter somehow. Now that he had someone waiting for him, he didn't like to be gone. And he sure liked the welcome she treated him to when he walked in.

"What exactly are you saying?" he asked.

"The hearings will cease."

"Good news." Luke started to get up.

"However—"

Holden nodded to Luke as he slid back into his seat. "Another 'however.'"

"Your group needs to come under the purview of the intelligence community."

Holden closed the folder and slid it back over to David. "You were making sense until right there. Now you're back to ticking me off."

David gave them a condescending head nod. "Let me explain."

Holden was done. He'd rather be home with Mia. Anywhere with Mia. "No."

Luke put his hand against the table in front of Holden. "Now, we can hear the man out."

"Thank you." David smiled. "We can bring you under an umbrella, mostly keep your group intact and figure out the best focus for your skills on other projects."

Luke didn't let him finish before he chimed in. "No."

"I told you," Holden mumbled.

David actually looked surprised. "This is a significant concession. You wouldn't need to apply for positions."

Holden thought about laughing. They'd just taken down a corrupt politician and David was talking about benefits and interviews with

Human Resources. "No. Luke's said it and now I have. No."

"And in case you're not clear, I agree with Holden." Luke cleared his throat. "No."

David glanced from Holden to Luke. "Clearly you've had some stressful moments over the past few weeks. Your former boss is missing and that does not help the situation. I understand that."

"I don't think you're getting this," Holden said.

"You need time to think over this proposal. I'll let you discuss it then get back to me."

This time Holden stood up and he didn't plan on sitting back down again. David was a less annoying version of Walters, but the plans for Recovery weren't any better coming from a man in a different suit. "The answer isn't going to change."

Doing his impression of a man who already held the congressional position, David ignored their comments and shook their hands. "I'll talk to you soon."

They almost reached the door when David spoke again. "And, Mr. Price?"

"Yeah?"

"Once this is my office, do not try to

break in here again because I will have you arrested."

Holden wondered if there was hope for this guy after all. "Understood."

AN HOUR LATER, Holden reached for a piece of pizza and said the words that most troubled him. "Steve Samson has been taken care of, along with the Congressman, but we still don't know where Rod is or if he's alive."

He felt Mia's hand move to his forearm. He never would have thought it possible, but that simple touch took most of the pain away.

"He was digging in something that caused a problem." Luke popped open a beer and handed it to Caleb.

"There's a limit on what we can do. We don't have the resources or the government behind us." That fact landed like a rock in Holden's stomach.

Claire took her husband's beer. "Only one of those is a problem."

Adam laughed. "You know something we don't?"

"You need money, right?"

Holden wished it were that easy. "It's more than that, Claire. It's about equipment and a secure place to work. We can't come in and out of your house."

"Oh, I agree," Claire said.

Mia rolled her eyes. "For smart guys they sure aren't picking up on hints very well. Claire, just tell them what you're proposing."

She gave Mia an imaginary toast with her bottle. "Leave it to a woman to ask the right question."

"I think we just were insulted," Adam said.

Claire didn't bother to deny it. "I can provide everything you need."

From the smile on Luke's face, Holden figured the married couple had been cooking something up. "Meaning?"

"My ex-husband died before I signed the financial agreement."

Luke dumped his pizza on his plate. "Can we talk about this without talking about him? Phil Samson is just about my least favorite topic in the world."

"After paying off his creditors and returning the huge sum he stole from his company's retirement fund—"

Mia slipped her arm through Holden's. "Classy guy."

He kissed her. "You wouldn't believe me if I tried to explain."

Luke raised his hand. "I'm still ready to find another topic. One that doesn't involve Phil Samson would be nice, so let's get to it."

Claire swatted at her husband. "The point is that I have money. It's Samson money and I don't want any part of it. My thought was to donate it to some cause that would drive the Samson family insane, but I think there's a better use for it."

Holden felt his heart's pumping skid to a stop. "You can't be offering what I think you're offering."

"We'll set up a corporation and fund it with my unwanted inheritance. Because of the problems with the government and the possibility you could be subpoenaed, you'll have to be even more careful. Private investigators have to follow the law."

"Or be good enough not to get caught," Luke said.

"And you have our first assignment." Claire looked around the table.

"Find Rod." Holden felt the tension ease from his gut. Having so many unfinished pieces was driving him nuts.

Mia had righted his upside-down personal life and given him a reason to get up in the morning and rush home at night. Claire's offer finished the puzzle. They could help other people and track down Rod.

Everything fit.

"Right. No matter where or how, our first priority is to find Rod and figure out what happened to those women in WitSec." Luke stood up and raised his beer bottle.

Soon they all raised a drink but it was Holden who spoke for all of them. "Then let's get started."

Holden was more than ready to move forward. With his personal life in order, he could focus again. Mia gave him that…and he would give her everything he could.

* * * * *

LARGER-PRINT BOOKS!

GET 2 FREE LARGER-PRINT NOVELS

PLUS 2 FREE GIFTS!

HARLEQUIN®

INTRIGUE®

Breathtaking Romantic Suspense

YES! Please send me 2 FREE LARGER-PRINT Harlequin Intrigue® novels and my 2 FREE gifts (gifts are worth about $10). After receiving them, if I don't wish to receive any more books, I can return the shipping statement marked "cancel." If I don't cancel, I will receive 6 brand-new novels every month and be billed just $4.99 per book in the U.S. or $5.74 per book in Canada. That's a saving of at least 13% off the cover price! It's quite a bargain! Shipping and handling is just 50¢ per book.* I understand that accepting the 2 free books and gifts places me under no obligation to buy anything. I can always return a shipment and cancel at any time. Even if I never buy another book from Harlequin, the two free books and gifts are mine to keep forever.

199/399 HDN E5MS

Name _____ (PLEASE PRINT) _____

Address _____ Apt. # _____

City _____ State/Prov. _____ Zip/Postal Code _____

Signature (if under 18, a parent or guardian must sign) _____

Mail to the **Harlequin Reader Service:**
IN U.S.A.: P.O. Box 1867, Buffalo, NY 14240-1867
IN CANADA: P.O. Box 609, Fort Erie, Ontario L2A 5X3

Not valid for current subscribers to Harlequin Intrigue Larger-Print books.

**Are you a subscriber to Harlequin Intrigue books and
want to receive the larger-print edition? Call 1-800-873-8635 today!**

* Terms and prices subject to change without notice. Prices do not include applicable taxes. N.Y. residents add applicable sales tax. Canadian residents will be charged applicable provincial taxes and GST. Offer not valid in Quebec. This offer is limited to one order per household. All orders subject to approval. Credit or debit balances in a customer's account(s) may be offset by any other outstanding balance owed by or to the customer. Please allow 4 to 6 weeks for delivery. Offer available while quantities last.

Your Privacy: Harlequin Books is committed to protecting your privacy. Our Privacy Policy is available online at www.eHarlequin.com or upon request from the Reader Service. From time to time we make our lists of customers available to reputable third parties who may have a product or service of interest to you. If you would prefer we not share your name and address, please check here. ☐

Help us get it right—We strive for accurate, respectful and relevant communications. To clarify or modify your communication preferences, visit us at www.ReaderService.com/consumerschoice.

HILP10R